Dead Simple

A QUICK READS COLLECTION

Mark Billingham
Clare Mackintosh

i dea
Library Learning Information

To renew this item call:

0333 370 4700
(Local rate call)

or visit
www.ideastore.co.uk

TOWER HAMLETS
Created and managed by Tower Hamlets Council

TOWER HAMLETS
Idea Stores & Libraries
WITHDRAWN

Mark Billingham is one of the UK's most popular crime writers. He is a former actor, television writer and stand-up comedian. His series of novels featuring D.I. Tom Thorne have twice won him the Crime Novel of the Year Award as well as the Sherlock Award for Best British Detective. Each of his novels has been a *Sunday Times* top ten bestseller.

Clare Mackintosh spent twelve years in the police force, including time in the CID, and as a public order commander. She left the police in 2011 to work as a freelance journalist and social media consultant, and now writes full time. Clare's debut novel, *I Let You Go*, was a *Sunday Times* bestseller and was the fastest-selling title by a crime writer in 2015. It was selected for both the Richard and Judy Book Club and ITV's Loose Women's 'Loose Books', and has been translated into 31 languages. In July 2016 Clare received the Theakstons Old Peculier Crime Novel of the Year award. Clare's second book *I See You* was published in July 2016 and is a *Sunday Times* number one bestseller.

James Oswald is the author of the Inspector McLean series of detective mysteries. The first two of these, *Natural Causes* and *The Book of Souls*, were both short-listed for the CWA Debut

Dagger Award. He currently lives in a large caravan inside a Dutch barn in Fife, with three dogs and two cats. He farms Highland cows and Romney sheep by day, and writes disturbing fiction by night.

Jane Casey is the bestselling author of *The Missing* and the Maeve Kerrigan series: *The Burning, The Reckoning, The Last Girl, The Stranger You Know, The Kill, After the Fire* and *Let the Dead Speak*. She has also written three crime novels for teenagers in the Jess Tennant series. She has won several major awards for her novels, which have been translated into many different languages. She is married to a criminal barrister and lives in London.

Angela Marsons is the author of Amazon number one bestseller *Silent Scream*. After years of writing relationship stories, Angela turned to crime, fictionally speaking of course. In Kim Stone she created a character who refused to go away. She lives in the Black Country with her partner, their bouncy Labrador and a swearing parrot.

Harry Bingham is the author of the Fiona Griffiths series of crime novels, set in Cardiff.

His heroine was described by the *Sunday Times* as 'the most startling . . . in modern crime fiction . . . brutal, freakish and totally original.' Harry – slightly less freakish than his creation – lives in Oxford with his wife and young family.

Antonia Hodgson was born and raised in Derby. She studied English at the University of Leeds. She is the author of the bestselling Thomas Hawkins crime series. Her first novel, *The Devil in the Marshalsea*, won the CWA Historical Dagger award in 2014. Antonia lives in London.

C.L. Taylor's first psychological thriller *The Accident* was one of the top ten bestselling first novels of 2014. Her second and third novels, *The Lie* and *The Missing*, were both *Sunday Times* best-sellers and Amazon Kindle number one bestsellers. She is currently writing her fourth psychological thriller which will be published in April 2017. She lives in Bristol with her partner and young son.

Dead Simple

Edited by Harry Bingham

First published in Great Britain in 2017
by Orion Books
an imprint of The Orion Publishing Group Ltd,
Carmelite House, 50 Victoria Embankment
London EC4Y 0DZ

An Hachette UK company

1 3 5 7 9 10 8 6 4 2

Copyright © for individual stories: *Hardscrabble*, Mark Billingham Ltd
2017; *The Funeral*, Clare Mackintosh 2017; *Dead Men Tell No Tales*,
James Oswald 2017; *Old Tricks*, Jane Casey 2017; *Tell No Lies*, Angela
Marsons 2017; *The Perfect Murder*, Harry Bingham 2017; *The Night Before
the Hanging*, Antonia Hodgson 2017; *Bird in a Cage*, C.L. Taylor 2017.

The authors have asserted their moral right in accordance
with the Copyright, Designs and Patents Act of 1988.

All rights reserved. No part of this publication may be reproduced,
stored in a retrieval system, or transmitted, in any form or by any
means, electronic, mechanical, photocopying, recording or otherwise,
without the prior permission of the copyright owner and the above
publisher of this book.

All the characters in this book are fictitious,
and any resemblance to actual persons, living
or dead, is purely coincidental.

A CIP catalogue record for this book
is available from the British Library.

ISBN 978 1 4091 6912 3

Typeset at The Spartan Press Ltd,
Lymington, Hants

Printed and bound by CPI Group
(UK) Ltd, Croydon, CR0 4YY

Tower Hamlets Libraries	
91000008014293	
Askews & Holts	
AF CRI	
THISWM	TH16001711/0006

Hardscrabble

Mark Billingham

Nobody knew why Kevin Connolly had smashed his cell up. There were plenty of people wondering. A few were making wild guesses, but nobody had any answers. Certainly, nobody was going to ask him the question.

There were a lot of questions you didn't ask in prison.

Up until three months before, he had been a model prisoner. One of the Governor's good boys. Serving his time quietly enough to earn himself a nice, cushy place on the Gold Wing. Bronze was basic, what everyone got when they came in. Silver got you a cell of your own with a TV, but Gold was... five star. A PlayStation and your own shower. En-suite facilities, for God's sake! Who wouldn't be happy with that?

Well, Kevin Connolly, apparently. Judging by the word from the screws in the know, who told of the mess he'd made. The sink smashed off the wall with a leg he'd broken off his chair. The bed turned into firewood and the shower tiles in a thousand bits and God knows *what* smeared up the walls.

So, after the usual 'you've let yourself down' lecture from the Deputy Governor, it was back to square one, but Connolly didn't seem too upset about it. A regular ray of sunshine, according to his new cellmate. He kept himself to himself, but he seemed happy enough. Nobody was any the wiser about why he'd done it, of course, or what he'd done to get put away in the first place. He never told anyone what he'd got up to on the outside, but that was his business.

It was respected, until such time as he chose to confide in someone.

Back with the everyday prisoners on Bronze, Connolly seemed a bit keener to muck in. It wasn't like there was much choice, now he was sharing again, but he put himself about a lot more. Woodwork classes in the Hobbit Shop once a week, GCSEs, and the rest. The highpoint of his day, though, according to the drug dealer he was sharing a cell with, was his regular afternoon game with William McDaid.

He never missed it, so the dealer said. Talked about it afterwards, the words he'd come up with, the scores, how close it was.

Connolly and Billy Mac playing Scrabble, for Christ's sake!

A seriously odd couple, that's what everyone thought. Pissing about, playing a stupid game.

Not that anyone would ever say that to Billy Mac.

They all knew what *he* was in for...

At two o'clock, when Connolly pushed through the open door of the cell, McDaid was already sitting, ready to start. The board was set up, square in the middle of the table. The wooden racks, one on either side. The green bag of tiles.

'Ready for another pasting?' McDaid asked.

'It was close yesterday,' Connolly said.

McDaid smiled. 'Right... close.'

Close, but McDaid had still come out on top. He usually did, to be fair. Even the rare times when Connolly sneaked a win, he suspected that McDaid had gone easy on him. Maybe McDaid thought that if he always won, Connolly might lose interest.

'Usual stakes?'

'Course,' Connolly said, grinning.

They knew what everyone thought, that they must be playing for something. For tobacco, for a few pennies or for... other things. Fact was, they played because they enjoyed the game and

3

the chat that went with it for an hour. Nothing at stake except for bragging rights.

'Not done much bragging last few weeks,' McDaid said.

Connolly walked across and pulled back his chair. 'Today's going to be different.'

'Really.' McDaid watched him. 'You brought your A-game?'

'Wait and see.' Connolly reached into the bag and pulled out his tiles.

Bronze or not, McDaid had a cell to himself. Nobody questioned it, but then they kept quiet about most things where Billy Mac was concerned. Every prison had someone like him. There was always a top dog. The screws knew it too and seemed happy that there was a way of doing things, as long as it was keeping the peace.

A pecking order.

The beasts were at the bottom of course. Sex-offenders. Ex-coppers were only a notch or two above them, with magistrates, grasses and the other pondlife. They were the VPs – vulnerable prisoners. Then there were gangs, same as there were on the outside. The ones moving drugs and mobile phones, or the ones sticking together simply because they were black or white or Asian. There were burglars and murderers, people smugglers, all sorts, and sitting at the top were the armed robbers. Nobody knew why they were always the ones calling the shots. That was just the way of things inside. They were Robin Hoods, with sawn-off shotguns instead of bows and arrows. They didn't give what they stole to the poor, nothing like that, but they were robbing the rich and that was what counted. Armed robbers were kings of the castle.

And Billy Mac was no ordinary armed robber.

So, favours were done. The nicest cell and the cushiest jobs. Privileges given that others had to earn.

His own Scrabble set, for a kick-off.

McDaid took seven tiles of his own and arranged them on his rack. He began moving them around. 'You to go first today.' The rasp in his voice and the thick Belfast accent were enough to keep most people polite. If Billy Mac said 'I like your shoes,' most people would hand them over on the spot.

Connolly looked down at his letters. They weren't great, but they weren't terrible either.

H.T.S.E.R.E.Y

He shuffled them around, aware that McDaid was watching him.

E.S.R.Y.T.E.H.

He thought for a minute or so and then played SHEET for eighteen points. It was a shame to use his S, but he couldn't see what else to do. He took five letters from the bag, and looked to see what he had.

R.Y.G.Q.E.O.I. Typical. A Q was always useful, but not without a U to go with it . . .

McDaid wrote down the score, same as usual, then quickly took his turn.

'What the hell's "VIBIER"?' Connolly asked.

'Vibier. You know, more vibey. You know what a vibe is, right?'

'Yeah . . .'

'Like, right now you're giving off a very . . . confused vibe.' McDaid laughed and patted the dictionary that was always sitting on the table next to him. 'You can always challenge me.'

Connolly shrugged. He waited, then played GROVE for ten points.

McDaid laid down BRINK for twenty-one.

SAY.

ZOON.

'Oh, come on. Bloody *Zoon*?'

'An individual animal produced from an egg,' McDaid said. Connolly challenged, and McDaid showed him the word in the dictionary.

TIES.

WISP. Four moves each, and McDaid was already forty-four points ahead.

Connolly sat back. 'No wonder you know so

many stupid words.' He nodded towards the three shelves of books above the table.

'You read, don't you?'

'Yeah,' Connolly said.

'Well, there you are.'

'But . . . so many.' Not just fantasy stuff either, like most of the others read. The ones who could be bothered to use the library. Hardback books too, some of them. Science and history. *Politics*, for God's sake.

'You're not going to ask me how I find the time, are you?'

Connolly wasn't quite that stupid. 'Just not what you'd expect, that's all.'

'Makes perfect sense to me,' McDaid said. 'I want to be smarter when I get out than I was when I came in. You're doing a GCSE, aren't you?'

'Only drama.'

McDaid laughed. 'You want to be an actor?'

'Something to do,' Connolly said.

Whatever McDaid had said, it still seemed . . . odd. Billy Mac, with the tattoos on his fingers and arms, creeping from the neck of his T-shirt. A shaved head that showed every scar, and teeth like broken headstones. No, not odd, exactly. Like one thing not quite going with another.

Like a vicar balls-deep in a brothel, or a blind man playing table-tennis.

Connolly went back to studying his letters.

When I get out.

To those millions the police had never found.

When Connolly had played PAIL for twelve points, McDaid sat back and shook his head. 'Old McDonald,' he said.

Connolly smiled and rubbed his hands together.

It was a jokey code they had. Like Old McDonald's farm. E-I-E-I-O. It meant all McDaid's letters were vowels, which was worse than useless. He swore under his breath and swapped them for seven new ones.

'You just giving me a chance to catch up?'

McDaid smiled, tombstone teeth. 'Always better when it's tight,' he said.

'Like a lot of things.' Connolly laughed at his own joke and played QUEEN on a double word square. 'Twenty-eight,' he said.

McDaid nodded like he was impressed. He said, 'Catching up,' and wrote the score down. Then he said, 'Why you here, Kevin?'

'I like playing.'

'No. Why are you *here*?'

Connolly looked at him. 'You serious?'

'We've been playing every day for months,'

McDaid said. 'Time to be upfront, I reckon. You know what I'm in for.'

'Everyone knows what you're in for,' Connolly said.

'There you go, then.'

Connolly moved his letters around for a while. Outside the cell door there was the squeak of a trolley wheel. The cheers of a high-stakes pool game floated up from below.

'I was a copper,' Connolly said, quietly.

'Fuck off.' Not so quiet.

Connolly nodded and answered the next question before it was asked. 'I didn't want the VP wing. Not with the sort that's over there.'

McDaid nodded, like that made sense. 'Taking a hell of a risk, mate. If the word gets out, there's plenty going to be sharpening their toothbrushes.'

'I'm past caring,' Connolly said.

McDaid played ROCKET for twenty-six points. Connolly could do little but add an S and lay down STUN for seventeen. The lead widened.

'Bent copper, then?'

'Not at first.'

'We've all got to make a living,' McDaid said.

'I suppose.'

'You made a choice, same as I did.'

Connolly held out his arms. 'And here I am.

Doing a drama exam to kill the time, and listening to a drug dealer toss himself off every night.'

McDaid flashed a smile as he laid his letters down. 'Could be worse,' he said. FICTION scored him another twenty-four points.

Connolly groaned as he studied the poor choice of letters in front of him.

'Took some balls,' McDaid said, sitting back. 'Telling me that.'

'Like you said, time to be upfront.'

'Still.' McDaid stretched and yawned. He was pushing sixty, but the daily sessions in the gym had clearly paid off. The ink moved on his arms as the muscles flexed. His chest widened beneath the thin cotton of his T-shirt and the sinews bulged in his neck until he closed his mouth again. 'There's not too many would have.'

They played on in silence for another ten minutes or so. Connolly made up some ground with a few nice words. Then, McDaid used all seven letters to make HONESTY and his lead was over a hundred again.

'You had both the blanks.'

'Lucky,' McDaid said.

'That's it then. I can't win from here.'

'Course you can.' McDaid plucked new letters from the bag. 'Never know what's going to happen.'

Connolly looked at him. 'What about you then?'

'What about me?' He began to arrange the tiles in his rack.

'If we're being upfront.'

McDaid grinned. 'I'm an open book, Kevin. What you see is what you get.'

'You know what everyone thinks, right?'

McDaid let out a long sigh. 'That I stashed the money, you mean?'

Connolly nodded. 'And there's people looking after it for you.'

'Yeah, I heard that.'

'The two people who you did the job with. That's what someone told me. They're keeping it safe until you get out, because you never mentioned their names.'

'Why would I have done that?' McDaid looked at Connolly as though he was an idiot. 'Trust me, if I'd grassed them up, there'd be *plenty* of sharpened toothbrushes about. Even for the likes of me.'

'So, it's true then?'

McDaid leaned across the table and winked. 'It's your go.'

Connolly showed no sign of making his move. 'So, smarter when you get out and a damn sight richer.'

'I certainly hope so.'

'Once you've paid your two mates off.'

McDaid looked confused. Like a very bad actor *pretending* to be confused. '*What* two mates?'

Connolly smiled. A door slammed on the landing below. There was more cheering from the lads playing pool. 'There's a few names been mentioned, you know that?'

'What names are we talking about?' McDaid asked. 'Jack the Ripper, maybe? Lord Lucan? Shergar?'

Connolly waited.

'People love to make out like they know something,' McDaid said. 'When they know nothing.'

'It's natural, though, isn't it? To try and guess. To want to know something like that.'

'Do *you* want to know their names, Kevin?'

'What?'

McDaid leaned closer to him. 'Would it make any difference at all if I told you?'

Connolly looked down at his tiles. He began to move them around, but it was difficult because his hand was trembling. He said, 'Do you mean, would I tell anyone in here?'

McDaid lowered his voice and asked the question very slowly. 'Would it make any difference?'

Connolly shook his head.

McDaid nodded then sat back. Casually, he

said, 'Terry Bell and Gordon Janner. And it's *still* your go . . .'

A few seconds crawled past before Connolly pushed back his chair and stood up.

'You giving up?'

Connolly stopped at the door and turned. 'I wasn't lying when I told you I was a copper,' he said. 'I just forgot to mention that I still am.'

McDaid stared. He dropped a tile from between his fingers.

'I was actually part of the team that put you in here. None of the exciting stuff, just putting evidence together. Writing reports, that sort of thing. That was before I moved to the undercover unit.'

McDaid looked at the floor. His fists were clenched.

'A bit more exciting now, obviously. *This* . . .'

McDaid shook his head.

'Actually, I'll quite miss the Scrabble.' Connolly almost looked like he meant it. 'You never know, with a bit of luck one of your mates might end up in here. Someone new for you to play with.'

Connolly was opening the cell door when McDaid called him back.

'Actually . . . I wasn't being very upfront myself,' he said. 'When I told you it wouldn't make any difference, you knowing those names. Truth is, *Detective Sergeant*, I don't think you're ever going to forget them.' He began to move his tiles around. 'Right about . . . now, Terry Bell is outside your home address at 42 Hanley Gardens. Oh, and Gordon's over at St Mary's. That *is* where your daughter goes to school, right?' He looked at his watch. 'She'll be coming out any time now, I reckon. Don't worry, if your wife doesn't make it for any reason, Gordon's there to take good care of your little girl.'

Connolly leaned against the door for support.

'So, why don't you sit down and we can finish the game?'

Connolly walked slowly back to his chair. He looked down at the board and saw the word McDaid had made.

SCREWED.

'Another one to me, I reckon,' McDaid said.

The Funeral

Clare Mackintosh

The church is packed. *Standing room only*, people will say afterwards. I think of the last funeral I attended, where only the front three rows of the church were full. The undertaker had to shuffle into a pew to make up the numbers. Charlie would have been pleased with the turnout. I imagine him looking at the crowd, counting how many have come from the village, and working out who's travelled the furthest to get here. He'd be touched by (and perhaps a little smug about) the gentle sobbing coming from Elaine and the girls.

Everyone from the garage is here, their greasy overalls swapped for borrowed suits and shiny black ties. Charlie was a popular boss, never fussed about getting his hands dirty, even once he didn't need to. He'd give pep talks to the lads, telling them how he was once where they are, and how he built up the business from nothing. *And now look at me*, he'd say.

There's a noise from the back of the church. Everyone turns around, and for a second my breath catches.

We were married in this church.

Charlie waiting at the altar, turning round as I walked down the aisle, my dress a cloud of white silk.

Now I'm the one waiting for Charlie, in a black skirt, with a jacket hiding the way the waistband digs into my flesh. There are sniffs and swallows as the coffin passes each row of mourners. I catch sight of Charlie's cousin, all the way from Canada, and old Mrs Hobbs from a few doors down. They're both crying.

When it draws alongside me, I feel everyone looking at me. *So sad*, they're thinking. I catch sight of Tom, sitting across the aisle, and instantly look away.

Charlie's coffin is walnut, with a velvet lining. It was the most expensive in the catalogue, and even Elaine said it was too much.

'Your dad deserves the best,' I told her, and she cried again. She's only thirty – no age at all to lose your father, especially when your mother's long since gone. *I'm your wicked step-mother*, I used to say when she was tiny, and she'd hug me and tell me I wasn't wicked at all. I wasn't her mother, though. We both knew that.

They place him at the front of the church, where the vicar is waiting. He bows his head. The silence is broken by grief so raw I can almost taste it. Everyone loved Charlie.

Everyone except me.

I listen to the tributes with my head bowed, as though in prayer. I'm not praying, though. I'm looking at my good black shoes, and wondering if it's worth getting new soles for them. I'm wondering how many people might come back to the house for the wake, and hoping I've organised enough sandwiches. I'm wondering when would be too soon to clear the wardrobe of Charlie's clothes.

I'm wondering if anyone will ever find out what I've done.

When we stand to sing, Tom is looking at me. I can feel it. I turn a little, so I can see him. His face is solemn, and his eyes bright with the start of tears. He knew Charlie for a long time. Far longer than I've been on the scene. Theirs was an odd friendship – the self-made mechanic and the posh doctor – but it worked.

Elaine wanted a burial, but I told her Charlie had asked to be cremated. The truth is, it was me who wanted the cremation. Charlie never said. He refused to accept the truth, even when it was staring him in the face.

'I think I'm feeling a bit better today,' he said, although his cheeks were grey and his breath snatched.

You're dying, I thought to myself.

Tom came to the house, and I left the room to let them talk, knowing it might be the last time they did. An hour later he closed the bedroom door and set down his doctor's bag in the hall.

'It won't be much longer.'

The music starts and the curtains open. I hear a mechanical whirr, and then the coffin begins to slide slowly backwards. Someone cries, noisily. I hold my breath.

The curtains swallow Charlie's coffin, and he is gone.

Another prayer, and then silence. The vicar looks out at us expectantly, but no one moves. It's a moment before I realise no one wants to leave until I do. I wonder how long they would wait, and the thought causes a bubble of laughter to escape from my lips. I turn it into a cough, and feel the waves of sympathy from those around me, who think I'm struggling to compose myself.

Charlie was a good father. He wasn't a bad husband.

I just didn't love him.

The trouble with marrying for convenience is

that, sooner or later, you realise it'll never make you happy.

I stand outside the church, shaking hands with everyone as they leave.

So sorry for your loss.

My condolences.

He was a lovely man.

Elaine has composed herself enough to stand next to me. There are streaks in her make-up from all the tears she's shed.

'Thank you,' she says, for the fiftieth time. 'So good of you to come.'

Tom comes to express his condolences. His handshake is so fleeting I almost miss it.

'I'm so sorry,' he says to Elaine. She takes his hand.

'You were a good friend to him.'

'If I can be of any help,' he tells her, shrugging as if to say it would be no trouble at all.

'I worry about Sarah,' she says, as if I wasn't there. 'She's hardly slept since Dad died.'

'I could give you some sleeping pills,' he suggests, turning to me.

'Thank you, but I don't like taking pills. I'll be fine.'

'Will you join us back at the house?' Elaine asks, and Tom doesn't meet my eye as he replies.

'I'd be delighted.'

The wake seems to go on for ever. People tell stories, their laughter dying away when they see me; they feel too awkward to continue.

'Charlie would have wanted us to enjoy ourselves,' I reassure them, because that's what people expect. Elaine continues to cry silently as she clears glasses. She accepts sympathetic hugs from people we hardly know, and I begin to feel cross. I will have to keep in contact for a while, I suppose – people will expect it – but gradually we can drift apart. It's not as though I'm a blood relation, after all.

'Will you stay in the house?' someone asks me. A cousin, I think.

'I don't think so,' I say. I give a brave smile, hoping to prevent any further questions.

'Too many memories,' the cousin says.

Memories, yes. And the fact that, after Charlie's death, the entire house now belongs to Elaine.

'It's the house she grew up in,' he said when I queried the will. 'Her mother's house. You understand.'

'Of course,' I said.

And that was when it began.

Charlie thought I spent too much, flashing the cash on expensive lunches, beauty salons and designer clothes. He gave me money whenever I hinted at a shopping trip, peeling fifty-pound notes off the wad he kept in his pocket.

I'd come home instead with charity shop Chanel in the branded bags I kept expressly for that purpose, with a haircut that only cost twenty quid at Curl Up and Dye, and a spring in my step from an imaginary massage.

'High maintenance, my wife,' Charlie would say. He would roll his eyes pretending to disapprove, but secretly enjoying his status of 'provider'. I'd kiss him, tell him I loved him, perhaps even hint at what would be on offer later that night.

It was the least I could do in exchange for stealing his money.

The house is full of noise, and my head is throbbing. I walk into the garden and sit on the bench under the beech tree.

'Are you okay?'

I jump. Tom is standing by the hedge, a few metres away.

'Sorry,' he says. 'Stupid question. Difficult day.'

'Yes.'

He points to the bench. 'May I?'

I look at the house, at the French doors leading into the sitting room. *The drawing room*, Tom would call it. There are still so many people here. Anyone looking out will see us together. Rashly, I reach for his hand and pull him onto the bench.

'You shouldn't have come, you know.' I leave my hand in his, hidden between us. 'People will guess. They'll talk.'

'Let them talk. How could I leave you, today of all days?'

Tom. Wonderful, handsome, kind Tom. Eyes that crinkle when he smiles, which he does now, making my stomach flip and my heart lift. Never before have I loved someone the way I love Tom, and never have I been loved the way he loves me.

It takes time to steal a hundred thousand pounds.

Ten years, to be precise.

At first I wasn't even sure why I was taking it. What I was going to do with it. I just wanted it. If he wasn't going to leave me the house, he owed me this much, at least.

Two hundred pounds a week, more or less, stashed in a pillowcase at the back of the airing cupboard. *Enough to leave*, I thought, but I'd never been on my own before. I wasn't sure I knew how.

The day Tom kissed me everything changed.

*

'I'm so sorry. That should never have happened.'
He looked scared.

'Am I that bad a kisser?' I said.

He laughed. Relaxed a little, then closed his eyes like he was in pain. 'Charlie's been a good friend to me.'

We were standing in the kitchen. Charlie was at work, and Tom had dropped round to pick something up. We'd both felt it – that crackle in the air, like electricity. The kiss was everything I'd ever wanted.

'We can't do this,' Tom said.

I didn't answer, and a second later I was in his arms again.

He laughed when I admitted I had almost a hundred thousand pounds hidden in the airing cupboard.

'Do you know how much interest you could be earning on that?'

Not that much, as it turned out, but I invested it anyway. The money became my escape fund. My reward for a marriage I hadn't enjoyed; a prize to make up for a house that would never be mine. I watched the total rise like a child gazing at baking cakes.

We knew the current set-up had to change. Me

with Charlie. Tom with a wife and three kids. It wasn't making us happy.

We knew where we wanted to end up. A cottage by the sea; just Tom, me, and perhaps a dog or two.

We just didn't know how we would get there.

The answer came as we were lying in bed one afternoon, in a Travelodge on the outskirts of town.

'There's a drug,' Tom said casually, as though we were chatting about the weather, 'that has no taste when it's crushed up and mixed with food.'

My pulse quickened. I was lying with my head on Tom's chest, and I didn't move, not trusting myself to make eye contact with him.

'What effect does it have?'

'It's fatal,' Tom said. 'With the right dose. A sudden overdose, or something slower, given over a period of weeks.'

We fell silent, each deep in thought.

'A post-mortem . . .' I started.

'Well, that's the interesting thing,' he said. 'If a GP has seen the patient in the fourteen days prior to death, and can confidently declare the cause of death, there isn't a post-mortem.'

'I see,' I said.

And so a plan was made. Innocent white pills poured into a bottle that had held sleeping tablets; the label said two to be taken before bed. Two would be too many, Tom said. Instead I crushed a single pill into powder, then scooped a quarter into Charlie's tea. Simple. Effective.

I look at the house and see that people are leaving.

'You should go,' I tell Tom. He squeezes my hand.

'I hate to leave you.'

I want so much to be held. Instead he looks at me and very gently strokes the back of my hand with his thumb.

'Six months,' he says, 'perhaps less. Then we'll never be apart again.'

He stands and walks towards the house, turning to give me one last look before he goes. I catch sight of him briefly though the kitchen window, saying goodbye to Elaine, who is once again weeping into the dishwasher. I feel another flash of anger. That girl needs to pull herself together.

I sigh, and walk back into the house. The last of the guests are leaving, and I shake hands and accept hugs and nod and smile until they are all gone.

'Would you mind if I go and lie down?' I say to Elaine. 'I suddenly feel tired out.'

'Of course not. I'll bring you some tea.'

I feel a prick of guilt. *He would have died anyway,* I remind myself, *I've just brought things forward a bit.*

I go upstairs and lie down. On the dressing table there's a photo of Charlie and me on our wedding day. I close my eyes. Six months feels a lifetime away.

Elaine pushes open the bedroom door. I sit up and lift the pillows up, so I can lean back and drink the tea she's brought me. She's used my special cup, and laid it out on a tray with two chocolate biscuits.

'You didn't eat anything at the wake,' she said. 'I thought you might be hungry.'

'Thank you.'

She sits on the end of the bed while I sip my tea.

'I've put the girls to sleep in the end bedroom – I hope that's okay? They were tired.'

'It's your house,' I remind her. There's a moment of tension, while she tries to work out my true feelings. I force a smile, and she relaxes, relieved.

'It's yours too,' she says, 'for as long as you want it.'

We talk for a while, and I finish my tea and set the mug on the side. I lean back and close my eyes.

'I can't see me getting a wink of sleep tonight,'

I say, half to myself, although even as I say it, I feel a heaviness coming over my limbs. I open my eyes. Elaine is looking down at her lap, twisting her hands as though she's got something on her mind.

'Is everything okay?'

'It's important to get some rest,' Elaine says, 'it's been a difficult day for you.'

It seems an odd thing to say, and a sense of alarm creeps over me. 'Did you—' I start, but my lips feel like rubber and a thick fog begins to descend.

'Get some sleep, Sarah. We'll talk in the morning.' She stands up, turning to pull the covers over me. My eyelids are drooping, my hands like lead weights by my side.

At the door she dims the light. 'Don't be cross with me, will you? I know you hate taking tablets but you looked so tired, and I was worried.' She pulls the door until it's almost closed, her face in the shadow of the overhead light. 'I found some sleeping pills in the bathroom cabinet, and I popped a couple in your tea to help you sleep. I followed the instructions on the bottle.'

I try to speak, but she shushes me and closes the door, and the narrow beam of light shrinks still further, before it disappears altogether.

Dead Men Tell No Tales

James Oswald

Detective Inspector Tony McLean winced as he ducked under the police cordon tape. The elastic of his overalls pulled uncomfortably at his crotch and he had to stop a moment to adjust it or risk a painful injury. The crime scene bustled with forensic experts, but none paid him any attention. Then he saw a familiar face up ahead.

'What have you got for me, Sergeant?' he asked

'Young male, no ID so far. He looks foreign.' From any other policeman, the words might have sounded racist, but Detective Sergeant Laird, known to all as Grumpy Bob, was as fair minded as they came. He too was dressed from head to toe in white paper overalls, with paper bootees over his shoes and a paper hood pulled tight around his face. The forensic team was hard at work on a large black wheelie bin. It was chained to a nearby lamp-post as if it might run away. The lid was open and, as he approached, McLean saw a pale hand lying open across a bulging black bag. Stepping closer, he saw the rest of the body, dumped in the bin like so much rubbish.

The dead man lay on his back, staring up at the morning sky with blank eyes. McLean could see what Grumpy Bob meant about him being foreign. It wasn't as obvious as the colour of his skin or the set of his jaw, but something about that face suggested he hadn't been born in Edinburgh. He hadn't been born all that long ago either. A young life cut short.

'Do we know how long he's been in there?' he asked.

'They were all emptied yesterday, so not long. These things get used all the time, too. Probably dumped early this morning,' Grumpy Bob said.

McLean looked around the street. At this time of day it was quiet. The people who lived in the flats would have gone to work by now. The boutique shops at street level looked mostly empty.

'Who found him?' he asked.

'Cafe owner.' Grumpy Bob pointed to a nearby glass window, through which McLean could see a counter and a coffee machine. Most of the seats seemed to be occupied by police. He just hoped they were all paying for their drinks.

'We'd better go and talk to him then. Let forensics get on with their work .'

As he stepped away from the bin and the body,

McLean felt a hand on his shoulder, as if someone wanted to stop him. The fabric of his paper overalls was tugged back, tweaking painfully at his crotch again.

'What is it?' he asked, turning back. But there was no one there. A white-suited forensic worker stood on the other side of the bin, too far away to have reached him. He looked at the inspector and seemed puzzled.

'Did you want something?'

McLean shook his head. He must have imagined the hand. It had just been his paper suit not fitting properly. They never did. 'No, nothing,' he said.

The cafe owner introduced himself as Jon. He had the kind of beard that has to be looked after with hard work and special oils. It sprouted a good foot from his throat and chin in perfect dark ginger curls. He had swirling patterns tattooed on his neck and arms, which crept under his crisp white cotton T-shirt. He had a haunted expression, which after what had happened that morning was understandable.

'You run this place on your own?' McLean asked. They had sat down at a table at which a pair of uniformed constables had been sitting a moment before. It was remarkable how quickly all the police officers had left the cafe when the detective inspector had entered.

'Not normally, no. Wendy comes in twice a week, and Allan's usually here much the same hours as me, but he had to go to the doctor this morning. Bust his knee mountain biking in the Pentland Hills yesterday.' Jon said the names as if he expected McLean to know who he was talking about.

'So the man in the bin. You found him this morning? What time exactly?'

'Would've been about nine. I usually clean the place up a bit once the work crowd has eased off. You know, people heading to the office and picking up a latte on the way. I'd stacked the bags on the pavement, then went to put them all in the bin. Only, when I opened it up . . .' Jon swallowed. He lifted the tiny espresso cup in front of him and drank the contents in one gulp, his hand shaking the whole time. 'Someone must have put him in there overnight. He wasn't there yesterday evening when I shut up shop. I'd have called you then if he was.'

'Do you know who he is?' McLean asked. Beside him Grumpy Bob was jotting down notes.

'No,' Jon said. 'Never seen him before. If he was a customer, I'd recognise him. I never forget a face.'

'Really? Never?' McLean asked.

'Aye, it's a gift. See your lad in the white over-alls out there?' Jon leaned back in his seat and pointed to where one of the forensic workers was swabbing the side of the bin for evidence. 'That's Tom. He comes in here once or twice a month. I recognised a couple of the constables too. Cheeky sods thought they could get free coffee because it's a crime scene.'

McLean looked at his own cappuccino, half finished and not yet paid for. He reached into his pocket for his wallet and took out a ten-pound note as he stood up to leave.

'We'll need you to give us a formal statement. Detective Sergeant Laird will look after that.' McLean nodded at Grumpy Bob, who seemed quite happy to drink his own flat white without worrying about money. 'And I'm afraid your business is going to be rather slow until we've finished looking for evidence.'

Jon swallowed again as he looked out of the cafe window towards the black bin. 'I under-stand,' he said.

McLean handed him the tenner. 'Thanks for the coffee. And see you give DS Laird the names of those constables, okay?'

He headed out of the cafe, pausing at the door as he felt the lightest of breezes brush past his face. The dead man was being lifted carefully from the bin and placed in a body bag, ready for his trip to the city mortuary. For a moment McLean thought he saw something in the corner of his eye, someone standing beside him. But when he turned, there was no one there.

'Subject is male, Caucasian. I'd say around eighteen years of age. Generally healthy, although he shows some signs of having too little food at some stage in his life. Most obvious injury is a heavy blow to the back of the skull. It would appear to have happened before he died. It may well be the cause of death. Difficult to say whether it was deliberate or the result of an accident.'

McLean stood in the city mortuary, watching as his old friend Angus Cadwallader performed the post-mortem on the dead man found in the wheelie bin. They still had no ID for him, and no clues had been found at the crime scene. Or rather, far too many clues had been found there, as might be expected of a busy city street and a large bin shared by many businesses.

'He was dumped after he died,' Cadwallader said. 'The pooling of blood in the body suggests he was lying in a different position to how we found him. Probably for several hours.'

'So he was killed elsewhere and then his body

was brought to that street.' McLean spoke his thoughts out loud, staring at the naked body on the slab without really seeing it. 'That would suggest the death was accidental, certainly not planned. He was killed, then someone took their time thinking about how to dispose of the body. Or maybe just panicked and didn't know what to do.'

'Sounds about right,' Cadwallader said.

'But who is he? And where was he actually killed?'

'I just tell you how he died, Tony. It's your job to find out why.' Cadwallader shrugged, then turned back to the corpse.

'I know, Angus. But we're not going to get very far with this case until we find out. We've got nothing from missing persons. And if he's an illegal immigrant, I doubt the DNA database will turn up anything either.' McLean shook his head. 'We could really do with a clue or two.'

'Well, I'll do my best.' Cadwallader began examining the body again. He hadn't got far when the dead man's hand twitched.

'What the hell?' McLean jumped back in horror as the man's forearm rose slowly, bending at the elbow. The fingers of the hand flexed once, twice, and then with a dull metallic clang the hand slammed back onto the table. Cadwallader stepped in closer to the body. He put a finger to its neck to feel for a pulse, even though the man was quite clearly dead.

'Does that happen a lot?' McLean asked as Cadwallader picked up the dead man's hand and inspected it. Then he ran his fingers down the arm to the elbow as if looking for wires or some other kind of trickery.

'Eh? Oh, no. Don't think I've ever seen anything like it before.' Cadwallader paused, then put the hand back down and stared at the dead man's face. 'Still, there's a first time for everything.'

The street was very different a couple of days later when McLean returned with Grumpy Bob. The large bin had been removed. The space where it had been was now filled with piles of rubbish bags and cardboard boxes.

'Fancy a coffee, sir?' Grumpy Bob asked. The detective sergeant was well known for his caffeine habit and could never pass a cafe without going in. Looking in through the window, McLean could see Jon working behind the counter. Most of the tables were full, and the place had a nice, warm, busy feel to it. Clearly it had not been too badly affected by the grisly find in the bin outside.

'Hey. Mind where you're going, won't you?' He stumbled as someone knocked into him. He turned to protest. But there was no one there.

'You all right, sir?' Grumpy Bob asked from the cafe door.

'Thought someone bumped into me.' McLean was confused. He looked up and down the street. There were people about, but none close enough to have knocked him. Then he saw movement out of the corner of his eye. A man stood at the point where a narrow alley led around to the back of the cafe. He stared at McLean with angry eyes that glinted in the near darkness. Slowly he raised his arm, with his hand stretched out, and flexed his fingers once, twice. The inspector blinked, and the man was gone.

'Wait!' McLean ran to the alley, turning into it just in time to hear a clatter of falling rubbish at the other end. The man could not have run that far so quickly, surely?

'What's up, sir?' Grumpy Bob wheezed, out of breath from running to catch up.

'Did you see that man? The way he moved his hand?' McLean asked. Grumpy Bob looked confused. Clearly the answer was no.

'Never mind. Follow me.' He hurried down the alley, and came out in a small square at the back of the flats. He was just in time to catch a glimpse of a figure disappearing on the other side. By the time McLean reached that spot, the man was waiting at the corner of the next street, and once more he raised his arm and flexed his fingers. Then he disappeared, only to appear again further away a few seconds later.

McLean tried running, but he wasn't much fitter than Grumpy Bob, who was now a hundred yards behind. No matter how fast McLean ran, the man was always a bit further away. He flitted from shadow to shadow. But whenever McLean thought he would give up the chase and head back to the station, the man would appear just a little closer.

And then the man came to a halt. His face was shadowed by the light of a street lamp directly overhead. Behind him, a row of old garages stretched into the darkness. Some were open and empty. Others were closed, hiding whatever secrets were inside. McLean stopped too, taking a moment to catch his breath. Before he could speak, the man stepped backwards, through the nearest door without opening it, and disappeared.

McLean crossed the road slowly, looking for anything that might explain the man's disappearance. There was nothing. The garage door was solid. The little street was empty and silent.

'Getting too old for this, sir.' Grumpy Bob

gasped and clutched a hand to his chest as he caught up with McLean a few moments later. 'What are we chasing?'

'Ghosts, Bob.' McLean reached out and touched the garage door through which he had seen the man pass. When he reached down to try the handle, it was locked.

'Reckon there's something interesting in there?' Grumpy Bob asked.

McLean tried the handle again. The door was definitely locked. 'I guess we'll never know. There's no reason to get a warrant to open it.'

'Might as well go back and get that coffee then.' Grumpy Bob set off across the road, and McLean followed. He'd only taken two steps when he heard a loud click behind him. Grumpy Bob must have heard it too, as he stopped mid-stride.

'Did I just hear that?' he asked.

McLean reached back down to the garage door and grasped the handle. It turned easily this time, barely making a squeak as he lifted the door up on its runners. Taking his torch out of his pocket, he shone the light over the inside, half expecting to see the man cowering in the corner.

Instead the garage was neatly ordered, with metal shelves lining the walls and a clean patch of empty concrete floor in the middle. Clean, that was, except for the dark pool of spilled liquid clotting in the centre. Little flecks of white bone glittered in the torch light. Tufts of black hair and pieces of pale skin poked out of the mess like tiny islands in a dark red sea. McLean smelled the all too familiar scent of drying blood. He lowered the garage door back down again, as Grumpy Bob called in to the police station on his mobile phone.

'You reckon this is where he was killed then?' the detective sergeant asked once he had hung up. Somewhere in the distance, a wailing siren broke the silence.

McLean nodded, then let out a long sigh. 'I'll bet good money the blood matches our lad in the wheelie bin.'

It didn't take long to find the owner of the garage. McLean left Grumpy Bob on guard until back-up arrived, and headed around the corner to the nearest flats. Only one button on the door entry system was lit. When McLean pressed it, the front door clicked open without anyone answering the intercom. Inside, the door to one of two ground-floor flats stood open. McLean found a young man sitting on the floor in the hallway.

'I never meant to kill him. I just panicked.' The

young man's eyes were red from crying, his face pale and thin. McLean looked closer, recognising him as the forensic worker that Jon at the cafe had pointed out. Tom, that was his name. Perhaps this would explain why they hadn't found much evidence.

'Who was he?' McLean asked. 'What happened?'

Tom frowned, as if puzzled by the question. He reached up and wiped his nose on the back of his hand and sniffed. Then he flexed his fingers just as the dead man had on the mortuary slab.

'Why don't you ask him? He's just there.' Tom pointed to the other side of the hallway. McLean looked, and for an instant he thought he saw him, the dead body from the wheelie bin, staring back at him. He blinked, and the image was gone.

Flashing blue and red lights bounced off the side of the building, as two constables led Tom from the flat and sat him in the back of the squad car. A van from forensics had parked outside the garage and white-suited workers were examining the scene. There was none of the chatter between them and the police that McLean was used to, perhaps because the killer was a forensic worker himself.

'Did you believe him when he said it was an accident?' Grumpy Bob asked, nodding towards the squad car as it drove off.

McLean shoved his hands deep into his jacket pockets to warm them. The night had grown cold and they'd never got that cup of coffee. 'Doesn't really matter. It's a result either way.'

'And what are you going to tell the chief inspector when he asks how you found where the lad was killed?'

'I don't know, Bob. Maybe I'll—' McLean stopped speaking. He had been staring out into the dark where a small crowd of people had gathered beyond the police cordon tape to see what was happening. There weren't many of them, but one stood out from all the others. Pale, thin, he looked almost transparent in the flickering light. Slowly he raised his hand and flexed his fingers once, twice, before nodding at the inspector. Then he turned away and disappeared into the night.

Grumpy Bob's hand on his arm woke McLean from what felt like a dream, or a nightmare. 'You all right, sir? You look like you've seen a ghost.' McLean shook his head. A shiver was running down his back that was only partly due to to the cold.

'A ghost, Bob? Aye, something like that.'

41

Old Tricks

Jane Casey

Nina rang the doorbell and waited halfway down the path. A light came on in the hall. She got ready, shivering. She was only wearing a thin anorak, leggings, a T-shirt. Not enough for a cold night.

That was deliberate.

The man opened the door slowly. His face was pinched in the street light that flashed on his glasses, hiding his eyes. Grey hair slicked back, cardigan buttoned up, leather slippers, hunched shoulders. Old.

Old was good.

'Hi, I'm really sorry to bother you...' She stopped. There were men who liked her kind of prettiness, her skinny legs and pale skin, the halo of fair hair that was wilder than ever in the light rain that had started to fall. This old man wasn't one of them. His mouth was a thin line.

'I live at number twelve.' She gestured vaguely down the road. 'I've run out of money for the electricity meter, and I've got no light or heat. I can't cook dinner for my little girl.'

'Your little girl?' He leaned out to see. 'Where is she?'

'I left her with my sister. She's got no money either. I can get more tomorrow. I'll pay you back.'

'Why are you asking me?' His voice was harsh, as if he hadn't spoken for a while.

'There's no one home near me. I've been walking down the road, looking for someone. I saw your light on.'

'How much do you want?' he asked.

'Anything you can spare.' Ten pounds, she thought, daring to hope. Twenty?

He shook his head. 'I can't stand here. It's too cold. Come inside.'

Nina didn't want to go inside.

He stood back, holding the door open so she could see a narrow hall full of dark furniture, potted plants. It smelled of old person.

'I've got to get the money out. I don't want to leave the door open,' he said.

No getting around it. Money was money. She went up the steps. She would stay in the hall, get the money, and go.

Easy.

He shut the door behind her. Nina wondered

if she'd heard the key turn in the lock. She could understand him trying to stay safe. You had to be careful these days. You never could tell, she thought. Anyone could be waiting to rob you blind.

It was hard not to giggle, all the same.

'Here is my proposal.' He sounded less feeble now. 'I will give you one hundred pounds.'

Nina was twenty-two, but she'd been doing this a long time. No one had ever offered her a hundred quid before.

'What's the catch?'

'You have to stay in this house for one hour to earn it.'

'One hour?'

He pointed at a tall grandfather clock at the back of the hall. 'It's almost seven o'clock. That clock will chime seven times at seven o'clock. If you stay until it chimes eight times, I will give you one hundred pounds. Cash.'

'Is this a trick?' Nina asked, suspicious.

'Not at all.'

'I'm not doing sex.' Better to get it out there. She wouldn't, either. She never had and she wasn't going to start with this one. Though now that she was close to him, he didn't look so old. Fifty, she guessed, not really knowing. He was standing with his back to the wall, his hands down by his sides.

'You just have to stay.'

'Why?'

'Maybe I'm lonely.' The light was flashing off his glasses again and Nina couldn't really guess at his expression.

A whirring sound made Nina jump. The clock at the back of the hall started to chime. She counted along with it. Seven chimes.

She could do this – talk to an old man for an hour. For a hundred quid, she could do a lot of talking.

'All right, then.'

'Good.' He pointed. 'In there, please.'

'What's in there?'

'The living room.'

'Okay,' Nina muttered and started for the door, then stopped. She looked down at her scuffed trainers. 'Should I take these off? They're a bit muddy.'

'No.'

'But I don't want to get mud everywhere.'

'I said no.'

Nina swallowed. Maybe this wasn't such a good idea.

But a hundred pounds. It would take her days of knocking on doors to get that. If she was lucky.

And there was always the danger of the cops catching up with her.

So she opened the door.

The room was small and very warm, the fire blazing up the chimney. The only other light was a reading lamp shining over a faded, threadbare armchair. The walls were lined with books, hundreds of them. Big heavy curtains blocked out all the sounds and light from the street. Pictures covered every surface, fighting for space with stuffed animals in glass cases.

'It's like a museum,' she blurted out, then realised it sounded rude.

'Sit down.'

She perched on the edge of a lumpy sofa.

He crossed to a table with a tray on it: glasses, bottles, cut-glass decanters. 'Drink?'

'I'm all right, thanks.'

He stood and looked at her. The fire was behind him so he was dark, a shadow. Something about the way he was standing, though – it was different. More upright. More confident.

'I don't like drinking alone,' he said.

'Whatever you're having, then.'

She wasn't stupid: she watched his hands. She watched the liquid splash into the glasses, the same amount in each. It was the colour of honey and she could smell it from across the room.

He walked over and held out one of the glasses so she could take it.

'Can I have the other one?' she asked.

'They're the same.'

'So it doesn't matter if you give me the other one.' She stared up at him, not backing down.

'No. It doesn't.' He gave her the other glass. She had a strange feeling that he'd expected her to ask for it. She ran her fingers over the outside of the glass, over the pattern cut into it, then took a gulp that made her cough.

'It's very good whisky. Drink it slowly.' He put his own glass down beside the worn armchair. 'Some music?'

'Yeah. Okay.' She checked her phone while he was flicking through his records. Seven minutes past seven. God!

'So do you live here on your own?'

'Most of the time.'

What did *that* mean? Nina sipped her drink this time. It turned to heat in her mouth, spreading warmth down her throat, making her head sing. She squeezed her eyes shut and opened them again. She hadn't had lunch.

He found what he was looking for and slid the record out of the sleeve. He squinted at it, checking for dust and scratches, before he placed it on the turntable of a record player.

There was silence and then the first notes fell into the room: scratchy old violins. The sound swelled and Nina wanted to laugh. It was like nothing she'd heard before.

'What is it?'

'A Schubert quartet called *Death and the Maiden*.'

Nina wished she hadn't asked.

The man came back and sat down in his chair, turning the light away so he was still in shadow. All around the room, black unblinking eyes stared at Nina: a squirrel on a branch, a blackbird with its head tilted to one side. The more she looked, the more she saw. The largest case was full of tiny bright birds fluttering around wax flowers.

'Did you make these?'

He paused, his glass almost to his lips. 'A long time ago.'

'Nice to have a hobby.'

He gave a little bark of laughter. Nina didn't know why. She hadn't been being funny.

The music, the heat, the booze: it was all making her feel dizzy. She wanted to check the time again but it would be rude. She didn't want to piss him off before she got her money.

The money.

'Have you actually got the hundred quid?'

A nod.

'Can I see it?'

'You haven't earned it yet.'

'I just want to see.'

'You don't trust me.'

'I mean, I do. Obviously.'

'Or you wouldn't be here.' He crossed his legs. 'Unless you were desperate.'

'I am desperate. That's why I was knocking on doors.'

'Your little boy, so cold and hungry, shivering in the dark with your poor sister.'

'Yeah.' Nina took another gulp of whisky.

He reached into his cardigan pocket and took out a roll of notes. It was hard to see but Nina thought it had to be a grand. More. He counted off five and set them on the table at his elbow.

'There. You can look at it but don't touch.' He put the rest of the money back in his pocket.

Nina couldn't stop thinking about it. Two grand, she guessed. More.

It made a hundred quid look like not very much money at all.

She sipped her drink again, watching him. He was old. If she knocked him down . . .

No. She couldn't.

If she made him like her more, maybe he'd give her more.

49

She could ask.

What would she do for two grand? Nina knew very well, but she didn't want to think about it.

She felt too edgy to stay on the sofa. She jumped up to peer at the photographs on a side table. 'Are these your family?'

'Some of them.'

Black and white pictures. Old people. Stiff poses.

'Are they all dead now?'

'I suppose so.' He sounded amused. 'Do you like photographs?'

'Yeah.' She straightened up and found herself looking at a ferret, its tiny paws clutching a rock. 'I've got loads on my phone.'

'Your little one.'

'Mmm,' Nina said, seeing the trap too late. A mother would have loads of pictures of her kid, she supposed.

'Was it a boy, did you say?'

'Yep.' Nina couldn't remember now. Maybe she'd said a girl, before. But he didn't seem to care, anyway.

'What's his name?'

'Darren. After his dad.' Not that Darren would let her keep a baby.

'Why couldn't Darren give you money?'

'He's in prison.' It wasn't a lie.

'Why?'

Armed robbery, Nina thought. 'A mistake, that's all.'

Silence.

She sat down again. The music was creeping her out.

'Can I show you some pictures?' he asked.

'What kind of pictures?'

'Just some girls I used to know.'

'Girls,' she repeated. It was porn, obviously.

He looked almost young as he went to a heavy, carved cupboard in the corner and unlocked it. Nina checked her phone. Half an hour left. She couldn't stand it.

She had to.

He came back with a heavy album, black and fat. 'May I?'

Nina made room for him on the sofa, watching him out of the corner of her eye. Bigger than her. Not as old as she'd thought. There was a smell as he moved: something unhealthy. It smelled wrong. She tried to breathe through her mouth.

He leafed through the album until he found the page he wanted.

'There.' He held it so she could see: a girl with fair hair, lips parted in surprise, eyes wide. She was in a garden, in front of a tree with spring blossom.

'Who's that?'

'Her name was Sandra.'

'Was?'

'She died. In 1994.'

'I was born in 1994.'

'She was the first,' he said, as if she hadn't spoken.

'The first?'

He was looking for something else. 'There. Vivienne. Five years later.'

Vivienne was sitting on a chair – the armchair he'd been sitting in, Nina realised, but the fabric was brighter, not ripped. Dark hair, pale skin. She looked up at the camera, her face wary.

'Why isn't she smiling?'

'She was afraid.'

'Of what?'

He was turning pages again, pausing on one that made his mouth curl into a smile.

'Afraid of what?' Nina asked again and he turned to look at her.

'Of me, I think.'

Nina shot off the sofa. Her heart was thumping. 'What do you mean?'

He offered her the album. 'Don't you want to see Sarah? Or Beth? Beth was young, like you. She wanted to live very much.'

'You're *sick*.' She turned and ran for the door,

fumbling with the handle, feeling her heart thud.

He was coming after her. 'You've got to wait another twenty-six minutes to get your money.'

'Let me go!' She'd made it to the front door but it wouldn't open. She tugged at it, desperate. It was greed that had made her stay, greed that had made her ignore her instincts. Greed was going to get her killed.

'Are you sure?'

'Please.'

He held out the key to her and she snatched it, stabbing it into the lock, praying as she turned it that he'd let her go, that it wasn't a trick . . .

Night air. Freedom. She ran as fast as she could, sobbing, half-blind with terror. The street behind her was empty. He wasn't following.

But Nina didn't stop running until she was outside the police station.

She was halfway through the door when her brain kicked in. There was no point in trying to make a complaint. What could she say?

An old man scared me.

And what were you doing in his house? Nina asked herself.

Asking him for money.

Why?

I said I had a kid at home and no money for the meter.

And do you?

No.

Which is fraud by false representation. You're nicked.

Nina rubbed her wrists as if the handcuffs were already chafing them. No way. She couldn't say anything. Couldn't warn anyone. She wasn't a reliable witness.

She'd get herself into trouble.

And she'd had just about enough trouble for one night.

She walked away from the police station door, fading into the darkness as if she'd never been there at all.

He made sure the door was locked before he returned to his sitting room. He straightened the cushions and picked up the empty glass that had rolled across the floor. There was still a smudge of the girl's lipstick on the edge. He ran his thumb over it. Then he sat down to listen while the music played on. When the record ended, he lifted his telephone and dialled a number. It rang and rang but he waited patiently until the call was answered.

'Hello, Judith?' he said loudly. She was very deaf.

'Yes?' She sounded worried and a little out of breath.

'It's Philip from next door,' he yelled. 'Just wanted to let you know that girl was round again. The one who took money off you last year.'

'Oh no. Did she trick you too?'

'I rather turned the tables on her, Judith. I scared the living daylights out of her.'

'Oh, did you? How *marvellous*.' Then she said, a little uncertain, 'You didn't hurt her, though.'

'Would I do a thing like that?' Philip said and laughed when she did. 'I don't think she'll come here again.'

'You're my hero, Philip,' Judith said sincerely.

'My pleasure,' he shouted and wished her goodnight.

Dear sweet Judith, who had been so upset when she found out she'd been tricked. The girl had deserved to be scared with a little music and play-acting, Philip thought.

Actually, she had deserved much more than that. He raised his thumb to his nose to smell the fake vanilla of her lipstick. Then he licked it clean, slowly. Those narrow bones would have snapped in his hands like twigs, but she had spirit. She would have lasted longer than some of them. Judith was too deaf to hear screaming, luckily.

He'd always had good luck.

Philip sighed. Retirement was dull, but he had to accept that he wasn't quick enough or strong enough any more. He'd had his day. He had his memories. It was greedy to want one more.

He had wanted to scare the girl away, and he was sure he'd succeeded. But it was a shame, all the same, that she wouldn't be back.

Tell No Lies

Angela Marsons

I stand outside the building as the sun begins to set. There is a storm in my stomach as the fear and doubt lifts, and churns the half slice of toast I forced down for lunch.

Two police officers exit the building. They are full of energy and enthusiasm at the start of their shift.

They glance my way, curiously. The woman tries to make eye contact, but I turn my head to the side. She waits but I step away. Not until I'm ready.

They walk along to the squad car parked out front. I wait for them to drive away. It must be my decision. My choice. I will enter when I'm ready.

My hand curls around the single sheet of paper in my pocket. A rush of anger surges through me as I remember what I have read. That feeling pushes me towards the front door.

I take a deep breath and allow my lungs to exhale slowly. Now I am ready.

The drab lobby smells of something floral that does not mask the underlying smell of body odour. The wall is covered with too many posters. My eyes are overloaded with messages.

The officer behind the desk is unlike the officers I have just seen outside. He looks tired and I guess is getting near the end of his shift.

I approach the desk and he looks my way, a fleeting glance before he taps something urgent into the computer.

I step towards the glass panel that separates us. He looks again, closer, and frowns. His gaze moves to my left temple where the bruise is spreading. I can feel it itching and consuming my skin. The flesh around my eye has started to swell and block my vision.

I don't know how this works. Who goes first? Does he ask what I want or do I state my reason for being here?

'May I help...'

'I'd like to report...'

Our sentences cross. He smiles wearily at me and nods for me to speak first.

'I'd like to make a complaint,' I say, and instantly wonder if complaint is the right word. Why do I worry about things like that? I have a cut to the back of my ear, the skin around my eye is swelling by the minute and bruises are spreading beneath my clothes. Yet I'm worried about whether I've said the right thing, as though I will be tested later.

He nods in a friendly way and makes a call. I don't hear his words on the phone, but he asks me to take a seat. Before I sit down a door opens.

A woman wearing a plain white shirt and black trousers smiles and beckons me to follow.

Her eyes are kind behind thin-rimmed glasses. Her hair is long and dark, tied back in a ponytail that swishes as she walks. I try to match her confident stride as she guides me to an interview room that is like those in every television crime drama I have watched. It is windowless and grey with plastic chairs. On the table a tape recorder rests against the wall.

I sit.

She smiles at me, perhaps to soothe my nerves. I try to smile back but am not sure that I manage it.

There is a confidence in the way she moves, the way she sits, the way she reaches for a ballpoint pen and twirls it in her fingers. I try to recall if there was ever a time that I felt so assured.

She has an authority that is neither masculine nor aggressive.

I sense that she would never have allowed herself to be treated the way that I have been, and I can't help wondering why.

'Would you like to just talk before we begin?' she asks. There is a booklet to her right which she has not yet opened.

'Yes,' I say. Talking would be good.

She asks me about my marriage, my husband, my eighteen-year-old son. General questions that don't address either my reason for being here or her ability to help me. Again, I wonder if this is some kind of test. Is she wondering if I am a reliable witness? Will my story stand up in court? Is this the warm-up act before the main event?

Like before, I wonder if my answers are correct.

'Has he hit you before?' she asks, gently.

My hand tightens around the letter in my pocket. It gives me the strength to go on.

'Yes,' I answer.

'When was the first time?'

'Three years ago,' I say and the memory of the attack returns, as hurtful as ever. It was summer and it was just the two of us. Always, when it was just the two of us. Of course. I was cooking his favourite steak outside on the barbecue. I received a phone call telling me that my mother had been taken ill. The steak burned and he pushed me.

The next day he said sorry, and I readily accepted his apology. I was grateful for his apology. I wanted to thank him for saying sorry. I even went and bought more steak.

'And how long until the next time?' she asks.

'A few months,' I say. Four to be exact.

'Can you tell me what happened?' she asks softly.

'He came home drunk. I was asleep. He was banging into things downstairs. I heard something smash. I was worried. I thought someone had come into the house, a burglar, an intruder.'

I pause as I remember the scene. The nausea is rolling around in my stomach, but I have to say the words.

'My mother's vase, left to me in her will, was shattered on the ground. I was upset. I shouted as I bent to the floor trying to gather up the pieces, even though I knew it was pointless.'

'What did he do?' she asks, smoothly prodding me to say more.

I haven't realised that, although the scene replays in my head, she can't see what I can.

'He grabbed my arm and pulled me to my feet. And then punched me in the mouth.'

I see the distaste cross her face, and immediately I want to take the blame. I want to tell her it was my fault. What right did I have to question the actions of a grown man? So, he had been out for a couple of drinks and it had been an accident. It wasn't like he had picked up the vase and smashed it on purpose.

'How did you explain the injury?' she asks, perhaps realising that this was when I began to lie outright. The push after the barbecue had left no marks, but the punch to the mouth had caused me to tell lies.

I shrug. 'I told people I slipped over in the bathroom,' I admit, and I feel shame colouring my face.

'There are a lot of accidents in bathrooms,' she says.

I wonder why it is such a common excuse. Is there a chatroom somewhere on Facebook where tips of 'believable excuses' are shared? Is there an annual study group where one learns to hide the truth of what's going on?

'And what happened next?' she asks.

'He bought me flowers and said he was sorry.'

She nodded knowingly. 'And the time after that?'

'I hadn't ironed his work shirt,' I say.

'And your punishment for that crime?' she asks with a friendly smile.

'He pulled back my head by my hair and spat

in my face, and then kicked me in the back of the knee.'

I am surprised at the cold, but fair, manner with which I relay the most painful parts of my life. As the tension shows in her jaw, I realise that she is more upset than I am. But then I realise that what happened has been with me for much longer.

'You see the pattern?' she asks.

Of course I see the pattern. He hits me and is sorry. He hits me and is sorry. It's not a difficult trend to work out.

'Yes,' I whisper.

'Do you see something else?' she asks.

'Like what?'

'It's called escalation. Would you agree that each incident is worse than the last?'

I am trying not to hear any blame in her voice. Is she saying that I had the power to stop this happening? Does she think it is my fault too? Have I somehow made things worse by being so weak?

I don't trust myself to speak so I simply nod.

'What happened to bring you here?' she asks.

Will this memory be so easy to retell? The scene is much harder to recount as I have not yet properly processed it in my mind.

'I asked him if he was looking for a job. I knew as soon—'

'You are not to blame,' she interrupts me. 'None of this is your fault.'

I try desperately to believe her, and I carry on. 'As soon as I'd said it, I knew what was going to happen. I could tell by the look in his eyes.' How could a face that had once looked at me with such tenderness now regard me with undiluted hate?

'Go on,' she urges.

I swallow. Somehow this one will make it all real.

'He stood up and I tried to back away. I fell backwards over a pair of muddy trainers. He kicked me in the ankle and then again in the ribs. I kept trying to back away but he kept following me, kicking at my legs all the time. I couldn't move them out of the way, and he didn't pause long enough for me to be able to push myself to my feet.'

I can feel the tears gathering in my throat. It's not even the violence that claws at my heart. It is the hateful look on his face.

She encourages me to go on.

'He stood astride me. His feet were either side of my waist. He kicked at me as though passing a football from one foot to another. Left then right then left again. I couldn't back up any further as my head was against the stairs. And he knew it. He reached down and grabbed me by the throat and lifted me to my feet. Our faces were almost level, and I looked into a face that I did not know.

'His left hand dug into my shoulder, holding me in place while his right hand landed punches all around my body. So many, I couldn't keep up. I tried to defend myself, but it was as though he knew what I was going to do and kept beating me to it. When he was done I simply slid to the ground.'

I sit back, worn out. It is out now and I can't take it back. Another person knows everything that I have held inside for so long.

'And when did this assault happen?' she asks.

'At eleven o'clock this morning,' I say. Half an hour before I found the letter that has grown warm in my hand.

'You know that you're in danger?' she asks, gently.

I brush away the tears. Yes, for the first time I know.

She sits up straight. 'Okay, Mrs Mills. I'm going to get us a coffee before we carry on.'

I find her use of my married name strange. I have just revealed my deepest secrets to this woman. I've told her things that I've not shared with another living soul.

'Please call me Helen,' I say. For some reason that is important to me.

She smiles. 'And I am Maxine.'

'What happens now?' I ask.

'We start the process of helping you through this. I will ask you a lot of questions, and your answers will form my official report. They will not be easy questions, but I will be right here to support you. We will take photos of your injuries, and then we will bring in your husband for questioning.'

I pause before I nod.

She reaches across and squeezes my hand before leaving the room.

I take out the letter that has prompted my actions and force myself to read it again.

Dear Wendy,

I promise I will tell her this week. She must know by now that I no longer love her. Hell, most days I don't even like her. She has no idea how much she has changed, that her spirit is gone. She has allowed middle age to erase everything that was even remotely attractive about her. I cannot stand her near me. She is weak and not even a whole person any more. She has no backbone, no fire. After twenty-five years of marriage she sickens me. Even our son cannot stand her. You have been patient, my love, and after all these years of hiding, our time is almost here. By the end of the week we will be together and there is nothing she can do to stop us.

The letter is from my husband to my sister.

My purpose in coming today is to seek revenge for the acid he has flung at my heart. I want him to suffer.

I came here to help make the pain go away. To ease the aching in my soul. I came here to make sure that my husband would not walk away unhurt. I came here for reasons that were confused in my head.

I came here looking for revenge but, after listening to myself speak out about what I've been through, I no longer care for my pathetic stab at revenge.

I realise that what I really want now is justice.

Now I am angry. Now I am strong. Now I want to send the message that this is not acceptable, that I will not be treated this way.

Maxine enters the room.

I pull my shoulders back and take a deep breath.

'Maxine, I realise I've made a mistake,' I say.

Now she slumps into the chair while I sit up straight.

'Please don't be scared, Mrs . . . Helen. It has taken great courage for you to come here today. I know how hard this is, but I will be with you every step of the way.'

The disappointment weighs heavily on her face. How many times do women come to her, tell her their secrets? Share their pain with her, only to realise that they cannot go through with it after all.

I am not one of those women. Not any more.

I shake my head.

'No, I don't think you understand me. I don't want to withdraw my complaint. But I don't feel that I've made myself clear.'

I am surprised by the strength in my voice as I let go of the words that will change me for ever.

'The person you need to arrest is my son.'

The Perfect Murder

Harry Bingham

'Goodbye,' says my wife.

'Bye,' I say.

'There's supper in the fridge. Did I tell you?'

'Yes. You told me twice already.'

'Well then.' We kiss. 'Have a good time.'

We don't often have weekends away from each other. We've been married twenty three years and things get a bit routine, I suppose.

Anyway, my wife – Sally – is away this weekend with Janet, an old school friend. A trip to a posh hotel in Bath. 'Pampering ourselves,' she says, as though naming some well-known human right.

'Don't do anything I wouldn't do,' she says.

I smile, but I don't know why. What she said wasn't funny.

'And if you do get a chance to look at those gutters...' she says. 'They do need looking at.'

I smile again. The sort of smile that might mean anything.

She drives off. I close the door.

A whole weekend.

We've got two kids, both older teenagers. Both away till Monday.

I have the weekend to myself. Me and nobody else.

I make some coffee. Then – feeling bold – get a cigarette and smoke it in the kitchen. I don't smoke much, but I'm never allowed to smoke inside.

Ha! No one to stop me now.

I smoke the cigarette. Drop the butt in the sink.

I am a careful man and I generally follow rules, but it is nice breaking them now and again. The minor thrill of being bad.

A whole weekend! All to myself! What shall I do?

I don't know.

I mooch around. Fiddle through some old stuff. Old CDs. Ones my wife hates me playing.

I put on Pink Floyd. Play it loud.

The music takes me back to my school days. I start thinking about those days. All life ahead of me and . . .

Hold on! I remember I once wrote a list. 'THINGS TO DO BEFORE I DIE.'

I remember writing that list. I put ten things

down on it. Promised my best mate, Max, that I'd do them all.

Where is it now?

I've got a box of all my old stuff in the loft. I get it down. Wipe off the dust and open it up.

Love letters. From Claire, my first ever girl-friend.

She was sweet, actually, but laughed like a horse in bed. We went out for a few months, which felt like ages in those days.

But I'm not looking for Claire's letters. I'm looking for my list.

And here it is. A sheet of paper torn from an exercise book.

'THINGS TO DO BEFORE I DIE.'

Written in red pen, underlined twice.

Item one: 'Have loads of sex.'

I've ticked that box, more or less. I was never long without a girlfriend when I was younger, and my wife and I have always been okay in the bedroom.

I move on.

'Get a job I love.'

'Go to Amsterdam.'

'Have a massive music system.'

'Cycle round Britain.'

A job I love? Well, I'm a deputy head teacher. I'll probably make head teacher in the next few years. Do I *love* my job? I don't know. I certainly like it. I think I've ticked that box.

I've been to Amsterdam too, quite often. I love the place.

I've got a good music system.

I haven't cycled round Britain, but I don't really want to any more – and I did do a lot of cycling in my twenties. So yes, I've done as much as I need there as well.

And so on down the list, all ten lines of it.

Truth is, most of the entries aren't that interesting. And I've either done them all, or I've done them enough. As much as I want to. As much as I need to.

I'm a bit disappointed, really. I'd hoped I'd find something that gave me a surge of enthusiasm. A splash of youthful excitement.

And I realise: *That's what I'm missing!* A bit of excitement. I love my family. I like my job and my friends. But excitement? When was the last time I really felt excited?

I'm a man who cycles to work. Wears a suit and tie. Who polishes his shoes every Sunday, ready for the week ahead. I'm a man who keeps order. A rule-maker, not a rule-breaker.

I've made a whole load of sensible choices and ended up lost on Planet Sensible. It's not that

I don't like this place – but where's the excitement? Where's the thrill?

Then I realise that there's writing on both sides of the paper.

I turn it over.

And there it is.

Number eleven on the list of 'THINGS TO DO BEFORE I DIE.' In my neat schoolboy handwriting, I'd written, 'Commit the perfect murder.'

I only have to read those words to feel a little ripple of excitement gurgling all the way through my body. Starting in my belly and rippling out to the tips of my toes, the ends of my fingers.

Commit the perfect murder.

I've always loved classic crime fiction. Those books that are like beautifully made crossword puzzles, with a cunning little twist at the end.

You always end up thinking, *How would I have done it if I were the murderer? How would I have got away with it? Left no clue, no trace?*

Commit the perfect murder.

I won't do it, of course.

I mean, look at me. I'm a deputy head teacher with a stable marriage and two almost adult children. People like me don't go around killing people like... well, who?

Who would I kill?

I'm not saying I *will* kill anyone at all, but

just supposing I did. Just to fool around for a moment.

Who would I kill?

The answer's obvious. Back at school, when I was eleven, twelve, thirteen, there was a boy who made my life hell. Richie Sanderson, his name was. A horrible guy. I was smaller then. Wore glasses. Had these goofy teeth that didn't get straightened out till I was sixteen. And I was always the good boy in class. Neat. Careful. Getting my homework in on time.

And Richie? I don't know what his problem was. I think he was just mean. A horrible guy. The sort of person who pulled legs off frogs when he was six. Who made kids' lives awful when he was thirteen. Probably the sort of person who's gone all the way through life enjoying nastiness for its own sake. Making everything he touches horrible.

Richie Sanderson.

He once got a can of spray paint, held me down, and painted me pink. Hair. Face. A big squirted heart across my chest. A thick pink triangle at my crotch.

I was fully dressed at the time, but my school wouldn't let me go home to change, because my parents weren't there to let me in. The school treated me almost as though it was my fault

– and I didn't even dare name Richie Sanderson as the culprit.

He started calling me the Pink Princess, and the name stuck around for a good year or two afterwards.

'Hey, Princess,' he used to say, and I'd have to answer him or I knew there'd be worse things coming my way.

Who would I kill?

I'd kill Richie Sanderson.

Kill him happily. Kill him with pleasure.

I want to look him up on Facebook. Find him again.

I'm about to move towards the computer to do just that, when I stop myself.

The police can trace that kind of thing, can't they? First rule of the perfect murder is leave no traces.

The town library? They have computers. But they probably also have CCTV and sign-in books. That's no good.

An internet cafe? Maybe. But that's probably the sort of place the police know to check on. So I could just buy a computer for cash, right? Use it in a coffee shop. Ditch it when I'm finished.

I'm not saying I will kill Richie Sanderson – just...

Well, I owe it to my younger self to take this

idea a little further. And I owe it to my current self to behave like the careful, cautious man I am.

There's a second-hand computer place just down the road. On the way to the coffee shop.

Seventy pounds buys me a rubbishy old laptop, but it's all I need.

I drink a coffee and look him up. Facebook. Google. A few other sites.

It's not even hard.

Richie Sanderson – same ugly face, same loathsome guy – is now a sales supervisor at a carpet superstore in Kettering.

I don't have his home address, but I know which store he works at. He's uploaded a picture of his new car to Facebook. A silver Passat. And that's probably his house in the background. A mock Tudor semi.

Item Eleven. *Commit the perfect murder*.

Richie Sanderson.

I think of beating his face to a pulp, but quickly correct myself.

Too much blood.

I'm a reasonably fit guy and I weigh thirteen stone, so I'm hardly a pushover. But I don't like the idea of a man-to-man fight to the death.

I think about it a bit. Come up with an answer. A good, hard blow to the head, then choke him.

I wonder what to hit him with. A baseball bat,

that's the classic thing. Except I'm British and I don't like the idea of going all American.

So I think, *a bottle of booze*. A big one. An innocent thing to carry, after all. And I can strangle him with a length of electric cable.

Easy.

Sanderson looks like he's carrying a bit of fat. Not fit like me.

No one will ever suspect.

No one. When the police are called, they'll look for money issues. For jealous partners. For recent quarrels. No way will they think to go back thirty-odd years and dig around among ancient quarrels.

The Pink Princess.

Fuck you, Richie Sanderson, fuck you!

I'm not saying I *will* kill him. I'm just saying he'd deserve it.

But – though I'm *not* going to kill him – I do buy some more things. I buy (for cash, in a shop with no CCTV) a litre bottle of Jack Daniel's. Good thick glass. An excellent weapon.

Also a metre length of electric cable.

Leather gloves.

A cap with a sun visor. A T-shirt. Jeans. Shoes. A dark anorak.

Nothing like my usual style. I don't want to look like me.

I'm still not saying I *will* kill him. I'm not saying anything at all.

Except, okay, I admit it, I do drive to Kettering. Drive to that damn store. Park a few streets away – I'm still very conscious of not showing up on anyone's CCTV – and head for the car park.

My plan was just to hang around outside the store. Look like I'm waiting for someone. Only, it starts raining. Not just a light English drizzle, but one of those summer rainstorms when the sky seems to burst. The sort of shower which soaks you to the bone.

So I run into the shop.

I'm not being stupid, even now.

For one thing – did I tell you this? – I'm not planning to kill anyone. I just want to see how far this goes. Plus, I've got my cap pulled down. And anyway, I'm a man in my late forties. I look nothing like the frightened twelve-year-old I once was.

The store's horrible. Smells of new carpet, but *cheap* new carpet, you know. That gluey, nylon, toxic smell.

A pimply youth – not Sanderson – runs up, wanting to know if he can help.

'Yes, you can kill your boss,' I want to tell him, but don't. I say I'm just browsing.

I browse.

Riffle through horrible carpets. Swatches of beige nylon.

And then I see him.

Richie Sanderson. That hated face. He looks older now, of course. Sadder. But his mouth is still the same mean line . There's a dark frown line cut deep between his eyebrows.

He looks nasty. He hasn't changed. I bet he hasn't changed.

He has his coat on. An umbrella. He's heading outside.

I want to kill him.

I won't, of course.

'Want to' doesn't mean 'I will'.

But yes, I hate that person. I think I've hated him solidly for the last thirty years. That hate feels more solid than any positive feeling I can find for my wife, for my job, for my children, even.

The ripple of dark excitement that I was craving is urgent in me now. A black snake coiling inside.

I want to kill Richie Sanderson.

I follow him out of the store.

Follow at a distance. Cap down. The collar of my anorak pulled up.

The rain is still so hard that there's no one about. A few cars swoosh past, but they're hardly going to take much notice of two pedestrians hurrying in the rain.

Two streets, three streets, four. Then we get to a row of mock-Tudor semis. Houses just like the one in that Facebook photo.

This is where it stops, I think. These are the sorts of houses that belong to families. Husband and wife and two point four kids.

I wouldn't mind killing Sanderson. In fact, it feels okay to admit it now, I'd *love* to kill him. I really *want* to kill the bastard. But I'm me. A steady, careful, proper man. And I certainly wouldn't hurt an innocent wife. I wouldn't kill a father, no matter how much he deserved it.

Only then Sanderson rushes down a passage. Lined with privet on both sides, it's like a green tunnel leading down to someone's back garden.

It's lunchtime. I assume Sanderson has gone home for his lunch hour.

I go back to my car and wait two hours. More than enough time for him to eat his lunch and return to work.

Then I go back to that passageway to find out more.

The passage leads to a sort of studio flat. Small, damp and in the shade of a large beech tree. The place *is* in someone's back garden, but carefully screened by a wicker fence.

A divorced man's studio flat, I think. That's what this is.

A house for a man who lives alone.

I ring the doorbell. No one answers.

I peer in through the windows.

Messy. Beer cans. Plates lying unwashed in the sink.

A single man.

It's a pathetic life, I think. A school bully fallen to this. A horrible job. A horrible house. A failed life.

That doesn't make me less keen to kill him, however. Quite the opposite. I want to kill him even more. The fiery anger of my long-forgotten feelings returns as fierce as ever.

I want to kill Richie Sanderson.

And I do.

I do.

I wait until nine that evening. I walk down that little passageway. He's at home all right. Lights on. He's walking around in front of uncurtained windows.

I ring his doorbell.

He answers it.

I say, 'Richie, it's me.'

I say that, and smash him over the head with my bottle of drink.

The glass doesn't shatter and I hit him again.

Richie falls over. He's stunned, but definitely not dead. So I loop the cable round his repulsive little neck and pull tight, and pull tighter and keep on pulling till the loathsome little bastard is lying dead at my feet.

I drag him inside his own home.

Steal some stupid stuff. Stuff I don't want.

Some cash. (Fifty quid.) Some cards. (I'll ditch them.) A phone. (I ditch the SIM card and unhook the battery.)

Then turn the lights off, close the door and leave. Just walk back to my car – still parked a good distance away. Drive to a service station.

Change into my ordinary clothes in the gents' toilets. Pale blue shirt. Chinos. A sensible coat. Nice shoes.

The other clothes I just put into a plastic bag, then shove it into a dustbin.

Gone.

There wasn't much blood at the scene and I wore gloves throughout, but I wash carefully all the same. Both hands. Wrists. Face. Neck.

I'm not excited. I'm not flat. It's just one more thing done.

Ten 'THINGS TO DO BEFORE I DIE', and all of them done, even number eleven.

And you want a twist, I know you do.

You're expecting one. Hoping for it.

Maybe I dropped my watch at the scene? Or my car was illegally parked and got a ticket? Or, quite by chance, an old pupil of mine happened to see me in Kettering?

But no.

The twist is: there is no twist. I am a careful man and I made no mistakes.

On Sunday, I cleared the gutters. Mowed the lawn. Did some jobs.

When my wife came back, she kissed me.

'Well,' she said. 'I hope you didn't?'

'Didn't what?'

'Didn't do anything I wouldn't do.'

I smiled at that and confessed the truth.

'Yes, I did actually. I cleaned the gutters.'

And as I say that, I realise something else.

I do like my life. Love it even. But it lacks that dark little sparkle of risk. The glint of danger.

I've murdered once and enjoyed it. But my 'THINGS TO DO BEFORE I DIE' list has just gained an extra item.

Item Twelve. Murder again. Murder soon. And murder better.

The Night Before
the Hanging

Antonia Hodgson

Charles Simmons is ready for his death. He's imagined it in every detail. Tomorrow morning, the
hangman will throw a rope around his neck. His
lungs will burn as he fights to breathe. His legs will
kick the air. He will twist, and choke, and suffer,
while the crowd cheers below him. Then his soul
will fly free from its cage and rise up to heaven.

This is fair. This is justice. He killed a man.
Now he must face his punishment.

This is what Charles Simmons believes, the
night before his hanging.

By dawn, he will have changed his mind.

Samuel Fleet was not in the habit of saving
people – quite the opposite. But he did enjoy a
puzzle, and he enjoyed it even more if it taught
him something fresh about human folly. Charles
Simmons was a puzzle, without question. He was
also, Fleet suspected, a tremendous fool.

It was past midnight when Fleet arrived at Newgate prison. His cloak was left open to the winter chill. His boots and brown stockings were flecked with mud, his coat was shabby from neglect. Grey shadows ringed his eyes. His cheeks were covered in dark bristle. A friend would have said he looked tired, and troubled.

Fleet didn't have any friends.

He handed the guard a parcel of books, wrapped in thin paper and tied with string. 'A gift, for the governor.'

The guard rubbed his thumb over the package, the paper crinkling softly at his touch. This was not a gift – it was a bribe. Fleet's books were filled with erotic scenes, described in vivid detail. The pictures were even more vivid.

Fleet scratched a line into the visitors' book.

Samuel Fleet   Bookseller, Russell Street
Sunday 6th December 1722

A half truth. Fleet had other trades, other business – none of which he would mark down on paper.

He dropped the quill, splattering ink across the page. 'Where's Simmons?'

The guard rolled his eyes.

*

Charles Simmons was on his knees, in prayer.

He had spent the last two months locked in a filthy cell, one of twenty men crammed together with no light and no air. Three weeks ago he'd almost died of a fever. He had sweated and shivered on a stinking mattress while his cellmates stepped over him.

God had spared his life. Now he had one last night to prepare his soul for judgement.

Everything was for sale in Newgate prison. Two shillings for a bottle of wine. Twelve shillings for a woman, smuggled in by the guard. Simmons had bought something much harder to find. He had scraped together every last coin he owned to rent this quiet cell, hidden deep within the heart of the prison.

Peace. This was what he'd bought, for his last night on earth. Peace – soft and smooth as velvet.

'Forgive me, Lord,' he whispered, eyes closed. 'Forgive my sins.'

There was a sharp rap at the door.

He flinched, then sat back on his heels, furious. 'Leave me be!' he bellowed through the thick stone wall.

The key rattled in the lock, and then the door slammed wide.

A short, shabby gentleman stood in the doorway. He lifted his hat and gave a swift bow.

'Samuel Fleet, at your service.' His black eyes widened. 'What the devil are you wearing, sir?'

Simmons rose to his feet. He was dressed in a long white smock that fell loose to his ankles. He lifted his arms as if he were giving the room his blessing. 'This is my shroud. I wear it to show God that I am ready to meet Him tomorrow. Now leave me. I have no wish for company.'

Fleet grinned. This should be amusing. He asked the guard to bring a bowl of punch, and more candles. 'Don't spare the brandy!' he shouted, as the door clanged shut.

They were alone.

Simmons glared at him. 'I was promised that I'd be left alone. I paid for that.'

'I paid more,' Fleet shrugged. He built a fire in the narrow grate. 'You should sit,' he said, waving to the only chair, which was pushed against the wall.

Simmons ignored him, prowling about the cell in a seething temper.

The guard returned with the punch bowl, filled to the brim. Fleet rested it on the chair, lovingly, as a mother might settle a baby in its cot.

Once the guard had left, Fleet poured himself a glass and stood with his back to the fire, flames roaring behind him.

The two men stared at each other across the

narrow cell – prisoner and visitor. Fleet was nearing forty. Simmons was ten years younger and a head taller. The fever had taken most of his strength. Beneath his shroud, his body was thin and weak. *But I could still beat him in a fight*, he decided. And then wondered why on earth this should matter, here at the end of his life.

'So,' Fleet said, tilting his head at the white smock. 'You're prepared for death.'

Simmons drew back his shoulders. 'I welcome it! God forgives all, even murder. I will die and then I shall be reborn in heaven. Washed clean of sin.' His eyes gleamed with the purity of belief.

Fleet frowned. This was all most curious. He'd watched the murder trial at the Old Bailey. Simmons had pleaded not guilty back then, and defended himself with great passion. 'So you confess to the murder?'

Simmons shivered, and clutched his arms. 'I don't wish to speak of it.'

'You murdered Jack Fletcher,' Fleet persisted. 'Your brother-in-law. Killed him in a stinking alleyway, near St Paul's. Stabbed him three times, in a great frenzy.'

'Yes, I killed him!' Simmons threw up his hands, as if to protect himself from the horror of it.

'Remarkable,' Fleet murmured to himself. He

rested his empty glass on a stone ledge and folded his arms. He looked at the prisoner for a long moment, black eyes hard and steady. 'You're not a killer, Mr Simmons.'

'I am,' Simmons whispered. 'God have mercy upon me. I *am*.'

'No, sir – you are not. And I can prove it.'

Fleet's words stilled the room.

Simmons wiped his brow with a white sleeve, swayed a little on his bare feet. It was the heat of the fire, no doubt. The last traces of fever. 'Why do you say this?' he asked, in a wavering voice. 'Why have you come here?'

'Because I want to help you.' Fleet's thick brows lifted, as if surprised by his own words.

'No.' Simmons narrowed his eyes. 'You are a demon. Sent by the devil to distract me from my prayers.'

'Am I?' Fleet replied, mildly. He took out his pipe and began to stuff it with tobacco.

Simmons crossed to the farthest corner of the room. He placed his palms on the dank stone wall and breathed deeply. Then he turned back to face his visitor. His expression was cool, almost haughty. 'You believe I'm innocent.'

'I know it.'

'Then who killed Jack, if not me?'

Fleet blew out a long trail of smoke. He didn't answer.

'Damn you, sir!' Simmons cried. 'You must tell me, or I will hang tomorrow!'

'At last!' Fleet cheered, plucking the pipe from his lips. 'I have roused you from your slumber. Yes, Mr Simmons, you will hang tomorrow – and you should be raging at the injustice. You should be pounding at the door until your fists bleed! But here you are, begging God to forgive you for a crime you didn't commit. Dressed in a smock.'

Simmons covered his face with his hands, but it was no use. The peace he'd worked so hard to find had vanished. Perhaps Fleet *was* a demon. But he had smuggled hope with him into this quiet cell. Hope, and doubt, and a hundred questions.

Out in the prison yard, the clock struck one.

Simmons dropped his hands. 'You say you wish to help me...'

Fleet nodded, impatient. 'Yes, yes. But first we must solve this mystery. How on earth have you convinced yourself that you're guilty?'

'There's no mystery. I killed Jack. I remember the knife in my hand. The blood...' He shuddered.

'Courage, sir.' Fleet's voice became soft and soothing. 'Close your eyes. Think back to that night. Summon it to your mind. The stench of the alleyway. Your footsteps on the cobbles. There was a thick fog, was there not?'

Simmons nodded, eyes closed.

'You're standing in the alleyway. The night is cold. The fog sits damp upon your skin. Now... describe what you see, what you feel. Every step. Every detail.'

Simmons did as he was told. And in a heartbeat, he was back in the alleyway behind St Paul's. He could describe it to Fleet perfectly. The air was dense with fog, which had turned a luminous silver in the moonlight. It was late, and the street was silent. He could hear nothing but his own footsteps, and his breath, and the blood pounding in his ears. His heart was thumping against his chest. He was afraid.

Why was he afraid?

Someone was following him, silently in the shadows.

No, no, that couldn't be. That wasn't how he remembered it...

The memory dissolved into a fresh scene – the one that haunted his dreams. His brother-in-law Jack was lying on the ground. Simmons was kneeling over him, a blade in his hand.

'Please,' Jack begged him, his eyes bright with terror. 'Please don't kill me.'

The dagger swung down in a great arc. Simmons was clutching it so hard he could feel the hilt biting into the palm of his hand. He slammed the blade into Jack's chest. He felt the jolt of it in his arm. He pulled the dagger out and stabbed again. Three times in all. Blood was pouring from the wounds. It covered his hands. It sprayed onto his shirt and waistcoat. He could smell it in the air, taste it on his lips.

He dropped the knife and sat back, panting for breath. There was a throbbing at the base of his skull. He reached a hand to the back of his head and felt a large and tender lump. He must have knocked it in the fight.

'Must have?' Fleet interrupted, bringing Simmons back to the prison cell and to the present.

Simmons rubbed his eyes, the story dying on his lips. The memory had been so vivid. It was as if he had been sitting in the alleyway, his knife in hand. He'd fallen to his knees on the floor of his cell. The cold was seeping through the thin cotton of his shroud. 'We must have fought.' But he didn't remember a fight. Only the blade, and the blood.

'The fog was very thick that night,' Fleet said, after a pause. He scratched his jaw, his fingers scraping against the black and grey stubble. 'But when you think back to the murder, you see it clearly.'

Simmons frowned. It was true – he could picture Jack's death exactly. 'Perhaps the mist cleared for a moment,' he said, doubtful.

'At your trial, you said you remembered walking into the alleyway – then nothing.' Fleet paused again. 'Why did you want to kill Jack Fletcher?'

'He beat my sister. He broke her arm. He was cruel.'

'Yes,' Fleet agreed. 'He was.'

Simmons looked up, sharply. 'You knew him?'

Fleet poured himself a glass of punch, letting the idea settle in Simmons' mind. 'You threatened him in Moll's coffee house – the day before he was murdered.'

'I did . . .' Simmons pushed himself to his feet, thinking hard. 'I was used, then? Someone wanted Jack dead, so they killed him and threw the blame on me . . . But I was found in the alley, covered in blood. I remember the blade. How is that possible?'

'Because it's not a real memory.' Fleet smiled. He was pleased to have solved the riddle. It had been bothering him. 'How many times did you stab your brother-in-law?'

'Three times. May God forgive me.'

'Once.' Fleet held up a finger. 'He was stabbed once, through the heart. Send for the coroner, if you don't believe me.'

'But—'

'Rumour, Mr Simmons. It has a tendency to play with the facts. One stab becomes three. Especially once the story is printed in a news-paper.'

'There were witnesses! A young boy, an old Spanish woman.'

'Portuguese,' Fleet said, dismissing both with a wave of his hand. 'The guard told me you fell sick in here, a few weeks ago.'

Simmons nodded, frowning.

'He says that until then, you always stated your innocence. But when you woke from your fever – a miracle! God had told you to confess your guilt. And by *great chance*, your confession matched everything the witnesses had said word for word. Their stories had become your mem-ories.' Fleet raised an eyebrow. 'But how did they see you, in the fog?'

'I . . . don't know.' Simmons was breathing heavily. Everything he had come to believe was tumbling down around him. And in his heart, he began to believe. *I am innocent. This man will help me. He will save me from the noose.*

'Your mind has been weakened by illness,'

Fleet continued. 'A fever of the mind, as well as the body. Do you dream of killing your brother-in-law?'

'Every night,' Simmons whispered.

'Your dreams have seeped into the real world, sir. You've taken the stories from the newspapers and ballads and spun them into truth. The blade arcing through the air. The way you gripped the hilt so tightly. How you stabbed him once, twice, three times. And more than that...' Fleet was pacing now, caught up in his thoughts. 'Accepting your guilt brought you peace. Certainty. You killed a man, so you must hang for it. You begged for forgiveness, and God was merciful. How neat. How comforting. How much better than the truth.' Fleet's black eyes gleamed in the candlelight.

Simmons was trembling. 'What do you mean? What truth?'

'That God isn't listening. That we are alone. That you will hang tomorrow whether you killed Fletcher or not.' Fleet stopped his pacing. 'Well. I've disturbed you long enough, sir. I'll leave you to your prayers.'

'What? Wait!' Simmons stumbled forward. He clutched at Fleet's stained and fraying coat. 'Where are you going? You said you would help me!'

'And I have.' Fleet's lips curled into a wolf's smile. 'You've wasted all this time praying over a crime you didn't commit. There are still a few hours before dawn. Now you may spend them repenting your real sins.'

'My real sins?' Simmons cried, still clinging desperately to Fleet's coat. 'But I'm innocent. You said so! For God's sake – you *must* help me!'

Fleet ripped Simmons' hands from his coat and pushed him away, hard. Simmons tripped and fell to the floor. Fleet stood over him, his face perfectly calm. 'Jenny Drake,' he said, softly.

Simmons flinched. 'What . . . how do you know that name?'

Fleet sighed. 'I know every dark story in this city, Mr Simmons.'

The fire had almost burned out. The air in the cell had turned cold again. For a moment, Simmons doubted himself. He almost saw his own guilt. Then he looked away. 'I did nothing wrong,' he muttered, struggling to his feet.

Fleet didn't answer. If a man would not recognise his sins, what purpose was there in spelling them out?

A year ago, Charles Simmons had made promises to Jenny Drake – a trusting, unworldly girl from Dorset. She had let him into her bed, trusting him. Almost at once he had grown bored, and abandoned her. An old story, old and cruel. She'd fallen then, to the tavern, to the brothel, to the gutter. By the time Fleet met her, she was dying of the pox. She never reached her sixteenth birthday.

It was not the worst thing Fleet had seen in this city. Walk through the slums of St Giles and one might see a hundred Jenny Drakes, starving and suffering and dying. But he'd noticed her at the end of a long and terrible day, lying alone in the street. And as he'd watched her, it had struck him that – for all that he had lost – here was someone in even greater pain. So instead of walking past her, he'd stopped, and listened. He'd taken her up from the gutter and paid for a bed and a nurse. Then later, he'd paid for her burial.

Jenny Drake never asked for revenge. She forgave the man who destroyed her.

Fleet did not.

There was still a small cupful of punch left over. Fleet tilted the bowl and scooped the last of the deep red liquid into his glass. He drained it quickly, then moved towards the door.

'Wait, damn you!' Simmons snarled. His white smock was streaked with grey dust and ash, where he'd rolled on the floor. 'How did you know I wasn't the killer?' Even as he asked the question, he knew. He drew back. 'It was you,' he breathed. '*You* killed him.'

Fleet turned. And smiled.

With a great cry, Simmons sprang forward.

Samuel Fleet was shorter than his attacker, and older. He was tired, and drunk. He was also a trained killer. Stepping nimbly to one side, he grabbed Simmons' arm, twisting it behind his back until it wrenched hard in its socket. Simmons screamed. Fleet put a hand on the back of Simmons' head and smashed his forehead against the prison wall.

The fight had lasted no more than five seconds. Simmons sat in a daze on the floor. There was a deep gash over his brow where he'd hit the wall. He put a trembling hand to the wound. His fingers came away wet with blood.

Fleet watched him, impassive. He could explain why he'd killed Jack Fletcher, and how much he'd been paid for it. He'd watched Fletcher and Simmons in the tavern that night, fighting. Then he'd gone home, and worked out his plan.

He'd killed Fletcher hours before Simmons stepped into the alley. Knocked Simmons out cold before dragging Fletcher's body from the cart and placing it on the cobbles. Put the knife in Simmons' hand. Splashed him with fresh pig's blood. Stood there in the silver fog and smiled, satisfied, before calling the alarm. He was gone before anyone saw him. The boy witness was his nephew. The Portuguese woman was an old friend, who owed him a favour.

Fleet could explain all this to Simmons, but he didn't care to.

'Guard!' Simmons cried out, feebly. And then, louder, 'Guard!'

Fleet stepped closer. He picked up the empty punch bowl.

Simmons shrank back. 'You devil,' he hissed. 'You devil.'

It was not the first time Fleet had been called that. It would not be the last. He lifted the bowl and dashed it across Simmons' brow.

He walked back through the prison with the guard. Simmons had attacked him, he said. 'I had to knock him out. Poor fellow. He's quite lost his mind, you know. He thinks *I* killed Fletcher. Can you imagine?' When they reached the gate, Fleet tipped his hat. 'Enjoy the books.'

The guard smirked. 'Thought they were for the governor?'

Fleet winked at him, and stepped out into the night. Within moments, he was lost in the shadows.

*

Charles Simmons woke at dawn, covered in blood. It took him a moment to remember that today was hanging day.

He began to scream.

Bird in a Cage

C.L. Taylor

The nurse at the hospice told me that Dad's last words were, 'Make sure the birds are okay.' He didn't mention me. Maybe he thought I was still in prison. Maybe he thought I was dead. The nurse told me he hadn't made much sense in his last few days. He'd used what little breath he had left talking about the birds, and the fact he'd paid his cleaner to look after them.

I let myself into Dad's house using the keys the solicitor had given me. Most people go from prison to a halfway house in the city, not a comfy four-bedroom detached home in the suburbs. It was weird, seeing it for the first time. It had been Dad's home for over twenty years and I'd never even seen a photo of it. And now it was mine.

I don't know if Dad had forgotten to pay the cleaner, or if she'd simply stopped turning up, but the house was in a state. There was a thick layer of grease on the hob, hair on the carpet, and dust on every surface. The worst thing was the smell. It hit me as soon as I opened the front door.

I almost screamed when I walked into the conservatory and saw the birds. There were dozens of them, lying dead on the bottom of the aviary like a multi-coloured carpet made of feathers. It took me a couple of seconds to notice that a blue budgie was still alive. He didn't chirp when I walked into the room. He didn't move. He didn't even look at me with his beady black eyes. He just sat on his perch, as rigid as a clothes peg, and stared at the wall.

Mum used to have a canary called Bobby. He lived in a cage in the living room and he'd tweet and chirp all the way through my favourite programmes. I didn't mind. I liked the company. I didn't have any brothers or sisters, and I wasn't a popular kid at school. Tess was pretty much my only friend. No, that's not true. She *was* my only friend. Until Julia took her away from me.

Mum didn't write to me when I was in prison. Dad did. He said Mum was having a hard time coming to terms with what I'd done. She wouldn't leave the house or open the door. She wouldn't even open the curtains. Dad hoped that a move from Bath to Bristol would help her, but it didn't. She got worse. That's why he built her an aviary in the conservatory and filled it with birds. He said she needed something beautiful to look at that would take her mind off what had happened. It didn't work. Six months after I went to prison, she had a stroke and died. That made two people Julia had taken from me.

I didn't expect the aviary to be so big. It must be six foot tall, six foot wide and a couple of feet deep. There's loads of room for one bird to fly about, but the budgie doesn't move, even though I've unlocked the doors to the aviary and the conservatory. A cold breeze gusts into the room and I shiver. The budgie doesn't react.

I root around in the plastic bucket in the corner of the room and pull out a packet of bird food. I pour some onto my palm.

'Look! I've got food. Come on. Out you come!'

The budgie still doesn't move. I know that it's scared. I know that it's spent however many years locked in a cage. And I know what it's like not to have any friends left. But, unlike me, this budgie has never been outside. It has no idea how exciting and scary the world is. I've got memories. I can remember being five and building a snowman in the garden with Dad. I can remember being eight and learning to roller skate in the park with Mum. I can remember being seventeen and going camping with Tess.

We were having such a good time – paddling in the stream at the bottom of her granny's field, sharing fags, making each other laugh. And then Julia turned up and spoiled everything.

'Please,' I beg the bird. 'Please come out.'

It doesn't move. Perhaps it senses how dangerous life is outside the cage? A cat or fox could kill it, or it might struggle to find food and starve to death. But that's got to be better than dying in the cage, surely? At least it will briefly know what it's like to be free.

I duck down and step through the doorway to the aviary, carefully pushing away the bodies of the dead birds with the toe of my trainer, so I don't squash them. The budgie's feathers ruffle but it doesn't leave its perch.

I reach out a hand. 'I just want to help—'

A loud noise makes me jump.

The sound of the doorbell startles the budgie too. It flies from its perch to the other side of the cage, fluttering desperately against the mesh, then drops to the ground.

Ding-dong-ding-dong-ding-dong.

I yank the front door open, ready to take a handful of mail from the postman or to tell a charity salesman to come back another time. But it's not a stranger standing on the path looking up at me with a big beaming smile. It's someone I know very, very well.

'Hello!' she says in a happy, smiley way that sets my teeth on edge. She hasn't changed in twenty years, except for a few lines around her eyes and a bit of a sag to her chin. Still blonde. Still perky. Still false as hell.

'My name's Julia,' she says, holding out a manicured hand. I ignore it and she awkwardly runs the hand through her hair instead. 'I'm your local Beauty Box representative. I've recently moved to the area and I thought I'd introduce myself.'

She pauses and looks me up and down. Fear grips the base of my stomach. She's going to recognise me. She's going to see through the five stone of fat that I've piled on, and the hair that went grey almost overnight when I turned thirty-five. Then she's going to shout, 'Oh my God, Ursula!' and back away as fast as she can.

Julia's smile widens, as though encouraging me to do the same.

Smile. Cheer up, love. Look at the face on that. Bulldog chewing a wasp.

I heard it all in prison. And worse.

Why do people always tell you to smile? It's not like a smile will stop a policeman arresting you or a judge sending you down. It doesn't magically bring the people you love back to life. What have I got to smile about?

'So . . .' Julia stares at me, waiting for me to say something. Her toothy grin falters and she blinks. 'Does Beauty Box sound like something you might be interested in? If you've got a minute, I could tell you more. Inside maybe . . .'

She looks meaningfully at the dark clouds above our heads. Nice trick. I wonder if she always goes from house to house when it's about to rain. Most people would take pity on her and invite her in. But I'm not most people.

'Okay, well . . .' Julia's expression changes from hopeful to disappointed, and she takes a step backwards.

'Why don't you come in?' I say, opening the door wider. 'I'd love to have a chat with you.'

Julia wrinkles her nose as she enters the house. Her gaze flicks from the dusty skirting boards to the peeling wallpaper. She flashes me a wide smile as I catch her eye, but not before I've seen the look of disgust on her face.

'Would you look at the size of this lounge!' she says as I usher her into the living room. 'You could fit my whole flat in this space.'

A nicer person would try to hide their envy, but Julia's never been very good at that. What Julia wants, she gets. Like Tess's boyfriend, George. Apparently she held his hand at her funeral.

'Goodness, would you look at that fireplace. Is it an original?' Her gaze flicks towards the ceiling before I can answer. 'And you've got a ceiling rose too, and beautiful cornicing. What was it you said you did for a living?'

'I didn't.'

The base of Julia's neck colours. It's the only part of her that isn't covered with thick, beige foundation. She tries to hide her embarrassment by rooting around in her make-up box. When she turns back to face me, she's waving four tubes of foundation and a make-up brush.

'Hmm . . .' She crosses the room and peers at my skin. 'Is there another room we could go into? Somewhere with natural light?'

My heart double thumps in my chest, and I feel a strange mixture of fear and excitement. 'We could go into the conservatory if you'd like?'

Julia spots the aviary as soon as she walks into the room and a small gasp catches in her throat.

'Oh God.' She stares at the aviary open-mouthed. 'Are those dead birds?'

I nod, and the expression on Julia's face changes from shock to disgust. She used to look at me like that a lot. She'd hiss 'weirdo' if

I walked past her at school, and encourage the boys to throw things at the back of my head in science.

'Oh my gosh!' she says, as the blue budgie hops over the body of one of its dead friends. 'That one's still alive.'

'I know,' I say, but Julia ignores me.

She takes another step towards the aviary, then another. My heart beats faster and my hands twitch at my sides.

'Some people,' she says under her breath as she ducks her head and steps into the bird cage, 'shouldn't be allowed to keep—'

She squeals with shock as I shove her as hard as I can and slam the door shut.

'Open the door.' Julia weaves her fingers through the metal mesh and pushes on it but the padlock holds firm.

I shake my head.

'Please.' The expression on her face changes from anger to desperation. 'Just open the door.'

I shake my head again.

'Open the door!' She charges at the mesh with her shoulder but it holds firm. Dad was always very proud of his DIY. He didn't cut corners or use cheap material. He built things to last.

Julia kicks at the base of the frame and pulls

at the mesh with her fingers. It doesn't budge. 'Why are you doing this? What's wrong with you?'

'Two people died because of what you did.'

'What?' She stares at me as though I've just escaped from a mental health ward. Then her eyes widen and her jaw drops and she whispers my name. 'Ursula?'

I don't reply. Instead I walk to the conservatory door and pull it closed. The nearest neighbours are several hundred metres away. I wouldn't want to disturb them with too much noise. Not when I've just moved in. I close the shutters too and the room instantly becomes dark.

'You left me in the pub,' I say to the shadowy figure in the bird cage. 'I had to walk back to Tess's field in the dark. It took me an hour. Anything could have happened.'

'It didn't, though, did it?' Julia's glossy red lips draw thin as she sneers at me. 'You're still alive. Unlike Tess.'

'And whose fault is that?' I rush at the aviary, slamming my fists into the wire mesh. Julia jumps back, terrified. The budgie in the corner of the cage chirps in alarm.

'Me and Tess, we were having such a good time,' I say. 'And then you turned up with George and ruined everything.'

I was gutted when I saw George and Julia walking up the field towards us. It was one thing for Tess to invite her boyfriend, but inviting Julia was the worst kind of betrayal. She knew I couldn't stand her.

Julia was wearing a tiny vest top that showed off her massive boobs. George put her tent up for her, but he couldn't stop staring at her tits as she arranged herself on the grass so he got a good view. She knew he was looking and she loved it.

'Oh, look at George's big pole,' she said. 'I've got a hole you could stick that in, George.'

She couldn't have made it more obvious that she fancied him. Why Tess didn't thump her I didn't know. But, instead of being pissed off, my best friend had turned into some kind of Julia groupie. She stuttered and blushed whenever Julia talked to her.

It was Julia's idea to go to the pub. She had a fake ID, and she made a big show of the fact that her dad had given her a hundred quid that weekend. Everyone apart from Julia got pissed, and Tess was paralytic. At the end of the night George carried her to Julia's car and laid her down on the back seat. Julia told me she'd come back and get me, after she'd dropped off George and Tess.

I waited an hour for her to come back. Then I

got fed up and decided to walk. It was cold and raining heavily, and I had to keep jumping into hedges when cars sped towards me with their headlights on full. The further I walked, the more pissed off I got. There was no way Julia was going to get away with what she'd done to me. I didn't care how popular she was or how much everyone else worshipped her.

When I reached Tess's grandmother's house I saw a light on in one of the upstairs windows. I could make out the shadows of two people kissing behind the curtains. I was pissed off with Tess for getting it on with George, instead of making Julia go back and get me. She'd probably tried, I told myself as I marched up the field. And Julia had told her not to be a killjoy. 'Can't you take a joke?' That was always Julia's comeback if she said or did something bitchy.

As I got closer to the tents I lit a cigarette, but it did little to calm me down. I was sick of Julia getting cheap laughs at my expense. I was sick of everyone going along with it because they were too shit scared to speak up. Well, I wasn't, not any more.

I could hear her snoring away in her tent. How dare she just go to sleep? Anything could have happened to me. I could be dead for all she knew.

I kicked at the side of the tent and shouted at her to wake up.

She ignored me, so I shouted again.

It wasn't fair. She treated people like shit all the time and got away with it, because her dad was rich and she was good looking. My own best friend had laughed along when Julia had flirted with her boyfriend, right in front of her eyes. Why was everyone so stupid? Why could no one else see what I saw?

I thought that if I scared her, if she felt as afraid as I had when I'd walked back in the dark, then she'd say sorry. She'd realise that I wasn't someone she could mess with and she'd leave me alone. That's why I held my lighter to the bottom of the tent. I thought it would make a hole. Maybe burn a little bit and then go out.

I didn't expect it to go up in flames.

How was I supposed to know that George and Julia were the ones getting it on in the house? How could I know that Tess had woken up in the car and stumbled up the field and into the wrong tent?

I didn't realise. I didn't know. How could I have?

'You burnt your best friend to death!' Julia screams now, pressing up against the back of the

112

cage, so she's as far away from me as she can get. 'You're a weirdo.'

I close my eyes, just for a second. 'No I'm not.'

Her gaze flicks towards the budgie in the corner of the cage. As she darts towards it, the heels of her stilettos spear the dead birds on the floor. The bird chirps desperately as she squeezes her hands around its small body.

'Let me out, Ursula,' Julia says, 'or I'll break its neck.'

The bird goes still. It stares at me with its black beady eyes. I wanted it to escape. I wanted it to taste freedom. I tried to encourage it out of the cage, but it wouldn't leave. It's been locked up for a long time. And that can do strange things to your head.

'I'll do it. I swear,' Julia says.

'Go on then,' I say softly.

'You're bluffing.' A bead of sweat draws a pale line through her perfect make-up. 'You wouldn't let me hurt this bird.'

'Wouldn't I?' I say.

And there it is, spread across my face. A smile.

About Quick Reads

Quick Reads are brilliant short new books written by bestselling writers. They are perfect for regular readers wanting a fast and satisfying read, but they are also ideal for adults who are discovering reading for pleasure for the first time.

Since Quick Reads was founded in 2006, over 4.5 million copies of more than a hundred titles have been sold or distributed. Quick Reads are available in paperback, in ebook and from your local library.

To find out more about Quick Reads titles, visit
www.readingagency.org.uk/quickreads
Tweet us 🐦 @Quick_Reads

Quick Reads is part of The Reading Agency,
a national charity that inspires more people to read more, encourages them to share their enjoyment of reading with others and celebrates the difference that reading makes to all our lives.
www.readingagency.org.uk Tweet us @readingagency

The Reading Agency Ltd • Registered number: 3904882 (England & Wales) Registered charity number: 1085443 (England & Wales) Registered Office: Free Word Centre, 60 Farringdon Road, London, EC1R 3GA The Reading Agency is supported using public funding by Arts Council England.

We would like to thank all our funders:

LOTTERY FUNDED

Quick Reads has something for everyone

Stories to make you laugh

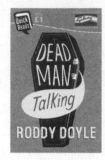

Stories to make you feel good

Stories to take you to another place

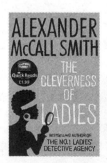

Stories about real life

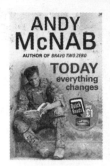

ANDY **McNAB**
AUTHOR OF *BRAVO TWO ZERO*
TODAY everything changes

Street Cat Bob
HOW ONE MAN AND A CAT SAVED EACH OTHER'S LIVES...A TRUE STORY
JAMES BOWEN

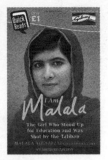

I Am **Malala**
The Girl Who Stood Up for Education and Was Shot by the Taliban
MALALA YOUSAFZAI

Stories to take you to another time

OUT OF THE DARK
ADÈLE GERAS

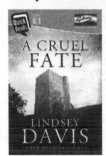

A CRUEL FATE
LINDSEY **DAVIS**

A DREADFUL MURDER
The MYSTERIOUS DEATH OF CAROLINE LUARD
MINETTE WALTERS

Stories to make you turn the pages

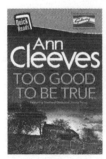

Ann **Cleeves**
TOO GOOD TO BE TRUE

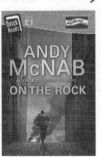

ANDY McNAB
AUTHOR OF *BRAVO TWO ZERO*
ON THE ROCK

WRONG TIME, WRONG PLACE
SIMON **KERNICK**
The No. 1 Bestselling Author

Agatha Christie
THE DOUBLE CLUE
Sophie Hannah and John Curran

For a complete list of titles visit
www.readingagency.org.uk/quickreads

Available in paperback, ebook and from your local library

Discover the pleasure of reading with Galaxy®

Curled up on the sofa,
Sunday morning in pyjamas,
just before bed,
in the bath or
on the way to work?

Wherever, whenever,
you can escape
with a good book!

So go on...
indulge yourself with
a good read and the
smooth taste of
Galaxy® chocolate.

Proudly supports

Read more at ⓕ Galaxy Chocolate

Galaxy is a registered trademark. © Mars 2017

Start a new chapter

One False Move

Dreda Say Mitchell

Hayley swore when she got out of prison that
she would turn her life around.

But living on the Devil's Estate doesn't make that easy.

She spends her days looking after her daughter, and her nights
collecting cash from people who can't get loans any other way.

But someone has just robbed her. And she has twenty-four
hours to get the money back, or her boss will come for her.

Her criminal ex-boyfriend says he can help.
Hayley wants nothing to do with him. But time is running out,
and she has to choose – save herself, or save her soul?

If she makes one false move, her life will be over ...

Available in paperback, ebook and from your local library

Start a new chapter

Looking for Captain Poldark

Rowan Coleman

**Four strangers, united by their shared love of
POLDARK, come together on a trip to Cornwall
in search of their hero . . .**

Lisa has sworn off love and relationships after a really
bad experience, but lately she's been tempted to take a chance
on a more exciting life. First she meets other fans of the
TV show *Poldark* online. Then she proposes a very
special road trip to Cornwall, in search of where
their favourite show is being filmed.

But can four strangers find friendship,
as well as a certain sexy hunk on their trip south?

Available in paperback, ebook and from your local library